How to Survive Summer Camp

How to Survive Summer Camp

Jacqueline Wilson

Illustrated by Sue Heap

OXFORD
UNIVERSITY PRESS

OXFORD

UNIVERSITY PRESS

Great Clarendon Street, Oxford OX2 6DP

Oxford University Press is a department of the University of Oxford.
It furthers the University's objective of excellence in research, scholarship,
and education by publishing worldwide in

Oxford   New York

Auckland   Cape Town   Dar es Salaam   Hong Kong   Karachi
Kuala Lumpur   Madrid   Melbourne   Mexico City   Nairobi
New Delhi   Shanghai   Taipei   Toronto

With offices in

Argentina   Austria   Brazil   Chile   Czech Republic   France   Greece
Guatemala   Hungary   Italy   Japan   Poland   Portugal   Singapore
South Korea   Switzerland   Thailand   Turkey   Ukraine   Vietnam

Oxford is a registered trade mark of Oxford University Press
in the UK and in certain other countries

British Library Cataloguing in Publication Data available

ISBN 978-0-19-272704-6

1 3 5 7 9 10 8 6 4 2

Typeset by AFS Image Setters Ltd, Glasgow

Printed in Great Britain
by Cox & Wyman Ltd, Reading, Berkshire

To Rebecca and Hannah Partos

Chapter One

I sat in the back of the car in my new T-shirt and my stiff new jeans and my pristine trainers and groaned. I kept dabbing at my new haircut. It felt terrible. Everyone would laugh at me. I thought about all these strange children at the summer camp. I peered down at the black lettering on my emerald green T-shirt. It said I LOVE EVERGREEN ADVENTURE HOLIDAYS. My new T-shirt was a liar.

'Are you all right, Stella?' Mum asked worriedly, turning round. 'Do you feel sick? You look a bit green.'

'To match my awful T-shirt,' I muttered, tugging at it.

'I think you look very fetching in your new outfit,' said Uncle Bill.

I didn't answer. I just pulled a face at his back. I couldn't stick my Uncle Bill. Which was a great pity, because he'd married Mum that morning.

I was the bridesmaid. Mum had bought me a

very expensive blue dress with puff sleeves and a long flouncy skirt. It had its own white lace pinafore and with my plaits undone and combed out Mum said I looked like Alice in Wonderland.

Only I didn't look like Alice at the wedding after all. I looked more like Humpty Dumpty, as bald as a boiled egg.

It was all a terrible mistake. Mum said I could go to a posh hairdressers and have my hair properly cut and styled the week before the wedding. She wanted to come with me but she had to work. I said I could go by myself, I wasn't a baby.

So I went after school and talked to this man called Kevin who looked like a rock star. He asked me how I wanted my hair cut. I decided I didn't want it too short. I measured a tiny amount with my thumb and finger. Kevin nodded and his scissors flashed. I screamed as they snipped. He hadn't understood. Before I could get away he'd snipped one side of my head to a stubble. He'd thought I wanted it that length!

He couldn't leave it like that, half stubble, half flowing golden corn, so he sheared the rest off. Mum cried when she saw me. Uncle Bill said he thought I looked cute, but he was only pretending.

I looked silly in the beautiful blue bridesmaid's dress at the wedding. I looked even sillier now in

my summer camp clothes. I was determined not to be really wet and cry, but I felt as if I might be going to all the same.

'Do try to cheer up a bit, darling,' said Mum, looking round at me again.

'Why should I cheer up?' I mumbled. 'It's not fair. You're going off abroad on your smashing holiday and I'm getting dumped in this horrible summer camp. I bet it'll be even worse than school. I know I'll hate it.'

'It's not my holiday, it's my honeymoon,' said Mum. But then she looked at Uncle Bill and whispered, 'Do you really think she'll be all right?'

I shook my head fiercely.

'Yes,' said Uncle Bill. 'Yes, of course she will. Most of my friends send their kids to summer camps and they all love it. They have a whale of a time.'

'I won't,' I said.

They didn't take any notice.

'I do wish all those other camps hadn't been fully booked,' Mum said. 'This Evergreen place does sound a bit . . . ' She searched for the right word.

I supplied it.

'It sounds a dump.'

'Now don't you be so cheeky,' said Mum, but she didn't sound cross, she sounded worried.

'I think it sounds a marvellous place,' said Uncle Bill. 'It's practically a stately home and it's got these huge grounds and a lovely swimming pool and—'

'Sh!' said Mum, but she was too late.

'I can't go!' I shouted. 'I can't go there, not if there's a swimming pool.'

'I promise you won't have to swim,' said Mum in her special you-can-trust-me tone.

But I couldn't trust Mum any more because she'd been mad enough to marry Uncle Bill.

'They'll make me. They'll throw me in,' I wailed, and I started crying like a baby.

Long ago when Mum was still married to Dad he had taken me swimming. I was only little and I was scared. Dad wanted me to jump in and splash and shout like all the other children. I didn't want to. I just stood on the side of the pool and shivered. Dad was kind at first but then he got cross. I got cross too so then he really lost his temper and threw me in. It was only the shallow end but it felt like Loch Ness to me. Dad hauled me out at once and laughed and tried to turn it into a joke, but I shrank away as if he'd turned into the Loch Ness monster himself.

I still had swimming pool nightmares. I'd never been swimming since.

'And you won't have to go swimming now,' Mum said, leaning over and dabbing at me with a paper hankie. 'I've written to this Brigadier who owns Evergreen. I've explained it all to him. No one's going to force you to swim, honestly. Anyway, you won't be *able* to go in swimming because you haven't packed a swimming costume, have you?'

'They could always make me swim in my knickers,' I mumbled tearfully.

I thought about the swimming pool at this summer camp. I imagined it very large, very blue, very cold. Then I imagined some sinister soldier man grabbing me and throwing me into the water.

'*Please* don't make me go.'

'Don't be so difficult, darling. You've got to go and that's that,' said Mum.

I didn't see why. I didn't see why I couldn't go to Europe with them. Mum kept saying I'd find it boring because they were just staying in cities and looking at lots of churches and galleries and museums, and anyway, it was their honeymoon. I thought they were much too old to have a honeymoon.

'Stop crying now, Stella. You don't want all the other children seeing you with red eyes, do you?' said Mum.

I used up three paper hankies blowing and mopping.

'Does it look as if I've been crying?' I asked anxiously.

'Not at all,' Mum lied. 'Hey, Bill—see those big gates on the right? I think we're there.'

I slunk down in the back of the car as Uncle Bill turned through the big gates and drove up the long gravel drive bordered by thick fir trees.

'It all looks very grand, doesn't it?' he said brightly. 'Look at all the Christmas trees, Stella. Why don't you sit up properly and see if you can see the house?'

I wriggled down further until my jeans nearly came up to my chin.

We turned a corner, the fir trees petered out, and here we were, at Evergreen. We stared at it in silence. It was great grey gloomy house with a tall tower at one end.

'It . . . it looks a little like a castle in a fairy tale,' said Mum desperately.

'No it doesn't,' I said. 'It looks like a prison. And I don't like that tower. I bet that's where they lock up all the naughty ones. Mum, *please*. Don't let them lock me up in this awful place.'

'Don't be silly, Stella,' said Mum, but she looked at Uncle Bill worriedly.

A big man came jogging round the corner of the house, a whistle bouncing up and down on his barrel chest.

'He'll tell us where to go,' said Uncle Bill, and he got out of the car quickly and called to him. The big man bounded across the drive towards us.

'Hello there. Welcome to Evergreen,' he panted. Little hisses steamed from his crimson nostrils.

'How do you do?' said Uncle Bill. 'Are you the Brigadier, by any chance?'

The big man shook his head, smiling.

'I'm the activities organizer,' he said. He spotted me cowering in the back of the car. 'You can call me Uncle Ron.'

I was sick of all these uncles. Uncle Bill forced

me out of the car to say hello. Uncle Ron patted me on my horribly cropped head.

'Welcome to Evergreen, sonny,' he said.

Sonny! I nearly died on the spot. He thought I was a boy.

'I'm a *girl*,' I said furiously.

Uncle Ron looked at me properly and then roared with laughter. His pale grey tracksuit was dark grey under his arms and he smelt.

'Sorry, Your Highness,' said Uncle Ron. 'What's your name then?'

'Stella Stebbings.'

'Ah yes. Stella. Jolly dee. Well, do you want to come through the woods with me to meet the other children? They're having a picnic by the poolside.'

'No thank you,' I said, backing away.

'We'd like to see the Brigadier first,' said Mum, getting out of the car and blowing her nose vigorously.

'I expect he'll be a bit tied up at the moment,' said Uncle Ron. 'But you can see his daughter, Miss Hamer-Cotton.'

There was a faraway sound of children shouting.

'Duty calls,' said Uncle Ron, and he jogged away.

Uncle Bill got my suitcase out of the car boot. Mum went up the steps to the front door and rapped the lion's head knocker. She beckoned to me but I stayed down on the gravel path. I turned my back and wrote in the gravel with my toe. I HATE EVERGREE . . . The door opened when I was halfway through the N. I quickly scrubbed it out before anyone could see. I now had one brilliant white trainer and one very grey and scuffed.

'Hello. Another new arrival at this time!' said an old lady in an orange overall. She shook her head at me. 'You're all behind like the donkey's tail. You've missed your picnic.'

'Can we have a quick word with the Brigadier, please?' said Mum.

'It'll be Miss Hamer-Cotton, dear. She takes care of all the new arrivals. This way, please.'

She led the way down the polished parquet corridor. My trainers squeaked and I left a little trail of dusty footprints. Orange Overall looked round and tutted, but she didn't say anything because I had Mum with me. I decided I didn't like her.

I didn't think much of Miss Hamer-Cotton either. She had very neat curled hair like rows of knitting and a powder blue tracksuit. It was meant to be baggy but her bottom filled it right up at the back. A little Siamese cat crouched on her shoulder and looked at me suspiciously. I held out

9

a hand to stroke him but he bared sharp little
teeth. I changed my mind about wanting to make
friends. Miss Hamer-Cotton had sharp little teeth
too. They showed a lot when she smiled.

'Welcome to Evergreen,' she said, shaking hands
with Mum and Uncle Bill. She just waggled her
fingers at me, and then plucked at her tracksuit
apologetically. 'Excuse my sports gear. I've been
organizing a few team races. We always like to have
lots of games the first afternoon and then a great
big picnic tea.'

I was glad I'd missed this famous picnic. I
wasn't a bit hungry anyway because of what I'd
eaten in the Wine Bar after the wedding. Mum

said I could have absolutely anything I wanted so I did. I had cherry cheesecake, Black Forest gateau, sherry trifle, chocolate mousse, and lemon meringue pie. I'd never eaten five huge puddings in one go before. By the time I got to the chocolate mousse I felt a little odd and I could only toy with the lemon meringue pie, leaving all the pastry, but I still reckon it was a considerable achievement.

Mum asked to see the Brigadier and Miss Hamer-Cotton explained he was hopelessly tied up right now and did we have any little problems we wanted to discuss? So Mum got started on Stella's Swimming Phobia and I blushed and fidgeted and felt foolish. Orange Overall brought in a big tray of tea and biscuits. The tea was almost as orange as her overall. The milk had separated into little white lumps floating on the bright surface. I only risked one sip.

The Siamese cat had his own special little saucer of milk.

'So he doesn't feel left out,' said Miss Hamer-Cotton. 'He's my special little boy, aren't you, Tinkypoo?'

I spluttered and Mum glared at me. She asked if she could meet the rest of the camp staff but they were all down in the woods with the children having their picnic. They sounded a bit like those teddy bears.

'Can we have a little look round the house then?' Mum asked.

So we went to see the Television Room. It contained a television. The Games Room wasn't very inspiring either. Two lots of table tennis took up most of the room. There were some school chairs and a little table covered with tattered comics that looked years out of date and a pile of board games and some lumps of very old grey plasticine that made the whole room reek.

'Of course the children only use the Games Room in very bad weather,' said Miss Hamer-Cotton. 'We keep them outdoors as much as possible. You wait till you see Stella when you come to collect her. I can guarantee she'll be as brown as a berry.'

'I don't go brown, I go red and burn,' I said.

'Can we see Stella's bedroom?' Mum said quickly.

'We put all the children in cosy little dormitories,' said Miss Hamer-Cotton. 'It's much more fun. We've put you in the Emerald dormi, Stella.'

The Emerald dormitory wasn't my idea of cosy. It had six little iron bedsteads straight out of a Victorian orphanage story, six little chests, and one green mat on the vinyl floor.

'We like to keep things simple,' said Miss Hamer-Cotton. 'Well, if you say goodbye to Stella now she can get unpacked before the other children come back from their picnic.'

Uncle Bill bent forward. I was scared he was going to kiss me so I edged away. He ended up kissing the air next to my cheek.

'Have a lovely time, Stella. Don't worry. You'll soon settle down. I'll look after Mummy for you and we'll send you lots of postcards.'

Mum didn't say anything at all. She hugged me very hard, gave me one big kiss, and then rushed out of the room. Uncle Bill went after her. Miss Hamer-Cotton said, 'This is your bed and chest, Stella. All right? See you later on, dear.' Then she went out too.

I was left all alone, abandoned at Evergreen.

Chapter Two

I sat on the end of my bed and stared round the ugly little room. I wondered what the other girls would be like. They'd all have made friends by now. My tummy went tight as I wondered what on earth I was going to say to them. My new jeans dug in so I undid the button. I hoped Mum had packed all my old comfy jeans too. I unsnapped my suitcase and stirred my clothes around a bit. I looked suspiciously for a swimming costume but there really wasn't one there. I found my old jeans and my shorts and my T-shirts and my rainbow jumper and one pretty summer dress in case we had to dress up for anything. Only I was going to look really silly in it now, like a boy in drag. Sonny!

I tipped my things out crossly, scattering them over the hard little bed. I dealt my clothes into the two top drawers of the chest and then squatted down to sort out my treasures. My new jeans still bit into my tummy even with the button undone. Perhaps I'd eaten one pudding too many. I wondered about changing into an old pair of jeans but I was scared these strange children might come bursting in and catch me in my underwear.

It was a relief spotting a doll sitting up on someone's pillow. I'd been worrying about Squeakycheese. He was a toy mouse that I'd had ever since I was a baby. He was a bit battered-looking now—blind and bald and he'd lost an ear and three of his paws—but I didn't care, I still loved him enormously. I'd hidden him inside one of my socks in case the other children laughed at him but I rescued him now and let him scamper on his one paw across my pillow.

Squeakycheese was my favourite toy. I'd taken my favourite book with me too, although Mum said it was much too precious. It was over a hundred years old and it cost ever such a lot of money. It was called *Fifty Favourite Fairy Tales* and the title was spelt out in very grand gold lettering on the blue leather cover. It was even more beautiful inside, with hundreds of pictures, lots of them in colour. There were flimsy tissue paper pages protecting all the colour plates, the sort that tear easily, but I'd not torn any of them even though I'd been looking at them ever since I was little, before I could read properly. I'd read all fifty of the stories now, some of them two or three times.

I found another book down at the bottom of the suitcase. It wasn't a reading book, it was a notebook with a red cover and gilt edges, the sort I'd been wanting for ages. There were more surprise presents tucked inside my nightie: a box of fruit gums, a big half pound bar of Cadbury's chocolate, and a new tin of felt tip pens.

I cheered up quite a lot. I undid the zip of my jeans, squashed up on my bed beside Squeakycheese, crammed a fruit gum of every flavour in my mouth, selected a felt pen, and started to write in my new red notebook.

I made up a story. It's the only thing I ever get a star for at school. This particular story was about a princess called Stellarina who had the most beautiful long golden hair right down to her waist. She'd been banished to an awful place called Everblack Castle by her wicked stepfather. I had great fun describing Everblack. Bats flapped in and out of the broken windows, snakes writhed around the cellars, and huge rats swam up from the sewers and paddled in the lavatories. Everblack was owned by a Brigavampire who lurked in his library until midnight and then rushed about slavering and baring his fangs. But he couldn't frighten Princess Stellarina. She rescued all these crying children from the Brigavampire and the wicked witch Hateful-Catty but just as they were all running down the drive a huge and horrible monster called Uncle Pong grabbed hold of Princess Stellarina and . . .

But I didn't have time to write what happened next. I heard voices and running feet. I shut my red notebook and shoved it under my pillow.

It was getting quite dark and I blinked foolishly when someone came rushing into the dormitory and snapped on the light. She was about my age. Maybe a bit older. She had long golden Princess Stellarina hair and an emerald green Ralph Lauren T-shirt and designer jeans and three real gold bangles on one slim brown arm. She would have been very pretty if her face wasn't screwed up in a scowl. I tried smiling at her but she stared at me as if I was an Everblack sewer rat. So I glared back.

Another girl came panting into the room. She looked younger. She had long fair hair too but it wasn't as long and shiny and silky. Her T-shirt was the Evergreen hand-out and her jeans were ordinary Marks and Spencer and the three bangles clacking on her arm were plastic.

'You won, Louise,' she gasped. 'You always do.' Then she saw me. 'Who's she?'

'Search me,' said Louise. 'She was sitting here in the dark when I came in.' She turned to me. 'What's your name?' she demanded.

I didn't see why I should tell her.

'Here, you.' The other girl came barging up to my bed. 'Louise asked you your name.'

I swivelled round to face the wall, ignoring her. I couldn't stand either of them.

'Leave her alone, Karen. She's been crying. The poor petal's homesick,' said Louise.

'I haven't been crying,' I said indignantly.

'Oh, it's got a tongue,' said Louise.

'Yes, and I can waggle it too,' I said, doing so.

'Why weren't you at the picnic?' said Karen.

'Because,' I said.

'We had races before,' said Karen. 'In teams. You're Emerald, like us. The other teams are Jade, Lime, and Olive. Emerald are best, aren't they, Louise? Louise won nearly all her races, she's brilliant at sports, so we got heaps of team points.'

Louise smirked and flopped on to her bed.

'I came third in the sack race,' said Karen. She leant right over me and picked up Squeakycheese.

'What's this old thing then, eh?'

'It's my pet sewer rat,' I said.

Karen shrieked and dropped Squeakycheese.

'You don't get toy sewer rats,' she said uncertainly. She started fiddling with the handles on my chest, opening the drawers one by one.

'You haven't got many clothes, have you?' she said rudely. 'You should see all Louise's things. She's got heaps of jeans and jogging pants and

18

shorts, and they're all designer too. And she's got three swimming costumes and a really grown-up bikini and a beautiful tennis dress with a pleated skirt and matching knickers and—'

'I'm not really interested,' I said, pretending to yawn.

'You're just jealous,' said Karen. She opened the bottom drawer where I'd put all my treasures. 'What's this book then? It's big enough.'

'You leave that alone. It's very old and very precious, so hands off,' I said quickly.

'It's fairy tales. How babyish! Who wants to look at a boring old book of fairy tales,' said Karen, pushing it to one side. She spotted my bar of Cadbury's. 'Ooh, chocolate, yum yum. Can I have a bit?'

I didn't see why I should share it when they were being so nasty to me, so I shook my head.

'Meanie. And fruit gums too. We're not supposed to keep food in the dormi. It's against the rules. Miss Hamer-Cotton said.'

'I don't care.'

'You're supposed to hand it in and then they give it to you a little bit each day, at tea. Louise had a huge iced cake and a great box of Belgian chocolate truffles. They're foreign and ever so expensive, at least . . . at least one pound each chocolate.'

'Karen!' said Louise from her bed.

'Well, nearly. Louise let me have a little bit and tomorrow at tea I'm getting a slice of cake, aren't I, Louise?'

'If she gets them back,' I said. 'I wondered why that Miss Hamer-Cotton is so fat.'

'You mean——? She wouldn't!' said Karen, falling for it.

'I can get more anyway,' said Louise, sitting up and stretching. Her gold bangles clinked delicately against each other. 'I'm going to write to my father to get him to send me a proper food hamper. If that picnic is anything to go by then the food here is disgusting.'

Two more girls came into the bedroom. They were both quite a bit younger than me. The littlest only looked about five. She was clutching a large toy donkey as if she could never let him go. Her eyelids were soft and swollen with tears and her nose was running.

'Hello. Can I have a look at your donkey?' Karen asked.

The little girl sniffed and ran to her bed. She lay down, tucking her knees up under her dress, the donkey draped round her like a stole.

'She's been crying,' said the other little girl, as if we couldn't work it out for ourselves.

'What's her name?' said Karen.

'I don't know. She won't say anything. And

she wouldn't join in any of the races. So I didn't either. Because we're friends.' She sat on her bed and swung her legs while she started undoing one of her little plaits.

'What's your name then?' said Karen.

'Janie.'

'Where do you come from, Janie?'

'Croydon.'

'No. I mean what country? You're black.'

'The Seychelles.'

'Where's that?'

'I don't know,' said Janie, shrugging. 'I've lived in Croydon since I was a baby.' She started on the other plait. 'Will one of you girls do my plaits for me in the morning? My mum does it for me at home.'

'I will,' I said. 'I'm good at plaits.'

'I bet you can't do proper plaits,' said Karen. 'You've just got silly skinhead hair.'

'You shut up,' I said. I'd forgotten my new haircut. My scalp prickled as they stared at me.

'Why do you have it cut like a boy?' said Karen. 'It looks awful. Doesn't it look daft like that, Louise?'

Louise shrugged. She undid her own hair and let it cascade to her waist.

'Oh, Louise, your hair is lovely,' said Karen. 'Can I brush it? Go on, let me brush it.'

21

Louise nodded graciously.

'Let's play hairdressers,' said Karen. 'I'll be the hairdresser and you can be a film star, Louise.'

'Can I play?' said Janie.

'All right. You can be another of my clients. Only you're not as pretty as Louise, so you can be just a lady.'

'OK,' said Janie. She went over to the little girl huddled beneath her donkey. 'Do you want to play hairdressers with us? I think it's quite a good game.' She waited. The little girl didn't say anything but Janie nodded. 'She doesn't want to play.'

I made out I didn't want to play either. I reached for my notebook and went on with my story. I made up two new people, a hateful proud princess called Lavatrise who had a horrible servant Kopykaren.

'What are you writing then?' Karen called, busy trying to wind Louise's long hair into a bun.

I tapped my nose and said nothing.

'That girl gets on my nerves,' Karen muttered. 'Who does she think she is, eh, Louise? She thinks she's great and yet she's awful. She's practically bald. Hey, Baldy! What are you scribbling, Baldy?'

They all giggled like idiots at my new nickname. I didn't even look up. I went on writing, taking no notice. I wanted to clutch Squeakycheese but

I thought that might make them laugh even
more.

The door opened and Miss Hamer-Cotton put
her head into the room.

'Hello girls. Having fun? Jolly good. It's nearly
bedtime, you know. I should start getting ready.
Aah, has the little one nodded off already?' Then
she noticed the donkey. 'Oh my goodness, that's
not a dog, is it? You're not allowed to have pets
here, it's strictly against the rules.'

'It's not a dog, Miss, it's a donkey,' said Janie.

Miss Hamer-Cotton came closer. 'Oh, it's a *toy*,'
she said, shaking her head. 'Really! You girls!' She
looked at us as if we'd played a trick on her. Then
she started counting us.

'I can only see five,' she said. 'Where's number
six got to, hmm?'

She went off to investigate and came back with
her two minutes later. She was older than me,
even older than Louise. She was a bit large and
lumpy but I liked the look of her.

'Here she is! She was only lurking in the lavatory
reading her book,' Miss Hamer-Cotton announced.

Karen tittered and the girl blushed.

'Don't be shy, dear,' said Miss Hamer-Cotton,
putting her arm round her shoulders. 'You'll soon
make friends. This is Marzipan, everyone.'

'Marzipan!' Karen spluttered.

I smiled sympathetically at Marzipan only she wasn't looking. I'd decided that she was going to be my friend.

Chapter Three

'Did you ever hear such a daft name?' Karen shrieked, the moment Miss Hamer-Cotton shut the dormi door. 'Marzipan! Did you ever!'

'She came last in all the races,' said Louise. 'And she kept missing the ball in rounders. Every time. Why does she have to be in the Emerald team? She's such a useless great lump. How old are you? Here, you. Marzipan. Don't say she's deaf as well.'

'What is Marzipan anyway?' said Janie. 'Is it little sweets like fruit? My mum bought some at Christmas once. There were little strawberries and apples and bananas, they looked ever so real. I played tea-parties with them but they got a bit sticky and my mum got narked.'

'What flavour of marzipan are you then?' said Louise. She stuck out her pink pointed tongue and pretended to lick her. 'Yuck! She's gone all sour and stale.'

'Keep away, she's gone rancid,' Karen shouted.

Marzipan walked to the empty bed and sat down on it. She opened her book and pretended to read it. I waited a minute and then went and sat next to her.

'What are you reading?' I asked. I looked at the title. 'Oh, *Little Women*. My mum keeps telling me to read that. Is it good?'

'Very,' said Marzipan in a tiny voice.

'*Little Women*! What a stupid title,' said Karen. 'I hate that sort of book. It's a boring old classic, isn't it? You can tell from the cover. I hate all them, they're boring boring boring, all long words and la-di-da. And girls who read them are boring boring boring too.'

'Don't take any notice of her,' I said. '*She's* boring. Do you want to see my best book?'

I showed her *Fifty Favourite Fairy Tales*.

'My mother got it in an antique market. It cost an awful lot of money.'

'It's lovely,' said Marzipan. She wiped her hands on her dungarees and took hold of it. She turned the pages carefully, pausing at the colour plates.

'Why's it got bog paper stuck in it?' said Karen. 'Here, let's see.'

I wasn't going to let her get hold of it and probably tear it, so I stuck out my foot and stopped her.

'She kicked me! Louise, did you see, she kicked

me,' Karen yelled. 'Right in my stomach. That's really dangerous. I'm going to tell on you, Baldy.'

'See if I care,' I said.

It had only been a little kick.

'It really hurts. I'm in agony,' Karen groaned.

'Don't worry. She's putting it on,' Marzipan whispered.

'I know,' I said. 'She's pathetic. Is Marzipan your real name?'

Marzipan nodded gloomily.

'My mother got a craving for it when she was pregnant,' she said. 'So she called me Marzipan when I was born. I wish she hadn't.'

'Oh well. It could have been worse. What if she'd gone crackers over Licorice Allsorts?' I said.

Marzipan laughed and I laughed too. We looked at my fairy tale book together. Karen went on with her hairdressing game while Louise sat staring at herself in her hand mirror. Talk about vain! Janie got fed up waiting for her turn and started doing handstands. The child on the bed made odd little sucking noises underneath her donkey.

'What's she making that funny noise for?' said Karen. She lifted the donkey. 'She's sucking her thumb,' she announced. She hesitated, but even Karen wasn't mean enough to tease her. 'She's only a baby,' she said, replacing the donkey.

Miss Hamer-Cotton got annoyed with us when she came back because we weren't in bed.

'This isn't a very good start, is it, girls? Come on now, quick sharp, get into your nighties. I'll be back in five minutes and I want to find you all tucked up, do you hear me? And don't forget to clean your teeth and pay a little call. Now then, no need to snigger. Come on, calm down. The other dormis are all settled and Uncle Ron tells me the boys are fast asleep already. We don't want the Emerald girls to lose a team point, do we?'

She hurried off. Louise ripped her Ralph Lauren T-shirt over her head and wriggled out of her jeans.

'Come on, you lot. I don't see why I should flog myself to death to win all the races and then get my precious team points taken away.' She pulled a beautiful white nightie over her head, trimmed with little pink bows and pink lace. A matching dressing gown lay at the end of her bed. She even had white slippers with pink ribbons and pink swansdown and little grown-up heels.

Karen was surprisingly bashful and undressed underneath her quilted dressing gown. Some of the quilting had come unstitched and it was a different blue from her pyjamas. When she was ready she begged Louise to let her try on her slippers. Louise let her have a little go. Karen couldn't walk properly in heels and her bottom stuck out.

'You don't half look daft,' I said. 'Doesn't she, Marzipan?'

But Marzipan wouldn't join in and tease Karen. Yet when Marzipan got undressed Karen made some awful remarks about her. I was glad when most of Marzipan was hidden under her long nightie. I told her I loved that Victorian style to comfort her, although I really liked my own red nightshirt much more. I reached up automatically to undo my plaits and it was a shock finding all the stubble. It felt shorter than ever. I pulled at it, willing it to grow a bit.

'Did you only just get it cut?' Marzipan whispered.

I nodded.

'It suits you. It's very stylish. Lots of fashion models have got their hair like that nowadays,' said Marzipan.

I felt a bit better—but perhaps she was only saying it to comfort me.

Janie looked very sweet in frilly white baby doll pyjamas and everyone made a fuss of her. She had a little blue toy teddy and her mother had made it a pair of frilly white pyjamas too. Janie showed the child with the donkey her blue teddy but she didn't seem interested.

'Hadn't she better get into her night things?' said Louise. 'Miss Hamer-Cotton will be back in a

29

minute. We don't really want to lose a team point, do we?'

'I'll undress her,' said Karen, but the little girl cowered away from her when she started to unbutton her cardigan.

'Don't. She's my friend, not yours,' said Janie. She hunched up beside the little girl, her frilly white bottom sticking up in the air. She whispered. The little girl said nothing but Janie nodded understandingly.

'She says she's very tired and doesn't want to get into her nightie. She doesn't want to clean her teeth or go to the toilet. She just wants to go to sleep, don't you?' She eased the little girl's shoes off and then pulled the bedcovers up to her chin.

We were all in bed when Miss Hamer-Cotton came back. She was pleased.

'There's good girls,' she said. 'Night night, then. Sleep tight. Sunday tomorrow. We've got all sorts of exciting things planned. There's swimming assessment in the morning and a hike in the afternoon.'

I sat up in bed.

'What is it, dear?'

'What's swimming assessment, Miss Hamer-Cotton?'

'Well, we have to sort out how far everyone can swim. Uncle Ron puts you through your paces and then you go in the beginner's class, or the intermediates or the advanced,' said Miss Hamer-Cotton, smiling. 'Now lie down, poppet, and—'

'But I won't have to go in the swimming pool, will I?' I interrupted.

'How do you think you're going to swim then, Baldy?' said Karen. 'Are you going to do the breast-stroke up and down the front lawn?'

'Now now. Don't be silly, girls. Lie down and we'll discuss all this in the morning,' said Miss Hamer-Cotton.

I couldn't wait until the morning.

'You promised I wouldn't have to swim! You promised! You know you did!'

'I don't know anything of the sort. I *do* know that if you don't stop talking to me in that rude tone of voice and lie down like a good girl I'm going to take off a team point straight away.'

'But—'

'Shut up and lie down, you fool,' Louise hissed.

I lay down and huddled up in a little ball. I wrapped my arms tightly round myself with Squeakycheese tucked into my armpit. I could feel my heart thudding against my arm. I shut my eyes to try to stop myself crying. It wasn't fair! She *did* promise. Well, Mum did. She swore I wouldn't have to swim.

'There, that's a sensible girl,' said Miss Hamer-Cotton, switching off the light. 'Night night, then. Straight to sleep and no whispering. I've got very big ears. Remember those team points.'

But we did whisper, of course, even Louise.

Karen kept asking me why I'd made such a fuss about swimming.

'It's because you're scared, isn't it? Do you hear that, Louise? Old Baldy's scared of swimming.'

'No I'm *not*,' I said. 'I'm just not allowed to, that's all.'

'Well, why aren't you allowed to? Go on, tell us.'

'You mind your own business.'

'See! She's just scared, isn't she, Louise?'

'Of course she is. Do whisper, Karen.'

'Scaredy cat. Baldy's a scaredy cat.'

'*Whisper.*'

'I can't go in swimming because of a serious medical reason,' I said desperately.

'You what?'

'You heard, ignorant. I have a serious—'

'Rubbish.'

'It's not rubbish at all. It's my heart. I can't go in cold water. My heart has this murmur and the shock could kill me.'

That silenced them. It silenced me too. I hadn't known I could tell such big lies. My heart thudded so violently I began to wonder if there really was something wrong with it. Squeakycheese nestled inside my nightie but for once he wasn't much of a comfort.

The others went on whispering for a bit and then they seemed to fall asleep. I lay awake for a long time, trying very hard not to think about swimming pools. The other girls made odd rustlings and mumblings. The old house creaked spookily. I wished I hadn't made up that story about Princess Stellarina and the Brigavampire. I kept thinking I could hear him creeping down the corridor. And there was another sound too, coming from a long way away. A wailing whimpering sound. I kept thinking I'd imagined it and then it would start up again.

'Can you hear a funny wailing noise?' I whispered to Marzipan, but she was asleep.

The wailing went on. Perhaps it was a child in one of the other dormitories. It must be a very young child, not much more than a baby. It sounded so sad. Perhaps it didn't understand about summer camp and thought it was stuck here at Evergreen for ever. It wanted its mother the way I wanted mine.

I sat up in bed and then slipped across the dormi towards the door. I opened it very carefully. The wailing grew a little louder. I stood there,

shivering, wondering what to do. Then a hand grabbed my shoulder and I shrieked.

'Sh! Shut up, Baldy.' It was only Karen.

'You didn't half give me a fright,' I whispered furiously.

'Well, what are you up to, creeping about in the middle of the night? You woke me up.'

'Someone's crying. You listen.'

So we both listened. Karen heard it too.

'I wonder who it is?' Karen whispered. 'Perhaps it's one of the boys? There's a very little one, only about three or four. I bet it's him.'

'Shall we go and find him?' I said.

'It's not allowed. We mustn't leave the dormi at night. Miss Hamer-Cotton said. Except in a case of emergency.'

'This is an emergency. Sort of. Come on.'

So Karen came with me.

'I think it's coming from the corridor on the right,' I said.

'Let's keep hold of each other. It's so dark. It can't be from down there. All the boys' dormis are back that way. So are the girls',' Karen whispered.

We stopped and listened again. It was quiet for a moment and I just heard a weird roaring in my ears—but then the wailing started again and it was unmistakable.

'It *is* from down there. Perhaps it's coming from

the tower,' I said. 'Yes, I bet Miss Hamer-Cotton's locked someone up in the tower.'

'She wouldn't,' said Karen, but she clutched hold of me. 'Let's go back to our dormi now.'

'But it's crying. We can't leave it.'

'Yes we can. And we're not allowed down there.'

'Well I'm going.'

'All right then. You go,' said Karen.

I hesitated, not sure whether I dared go on my own.

'Come with me, Karen. Please. Don't be such a coward.'

'I'm not a coward. You're the one who's a cowardy-custard, scared of a simple thing like swimming.'

We'd forgotten to whisper. A door suddenly opened somewhere down the forbidden corridor on the right.

'Quick!' said Karen, tugging me.

We ran back to our dormi, bumping into each other, frantic. I jumped into my bed with a great thud of the springs and then lay still, panting. I listened hard. There were no footsteps, no angry voices. And no crying. It had stopped.

'I don't think they heard us, Baldy,' Karen whispered.

'It's stopped crying.'

'Good.'

'Maybe it isn't good. Maybe they've done something to it,' I said.

'Don't talk rubbish. It's just gone to sleep.'

'Perhaps they've made it sleep,' I whispered. 'They could have drugged it. Or gagged it. Or smothered it.'

'Do shut up.'

So I did. I wanted to give Karen a scare but I was scaring myself too. I lay awake for a very very long time. Listening.

Chapter Four

I wanted to talk to Miss Hamer-Cotton without any of the others listening so I went along to her room when everyone else went down to breakfast.

'It's Stella, isn't it?' she said, stroking Tinkypoo. 'Downstairs now, dear. You don't want to miss your scrambled eggs, do you?'

'I've got to talk to you about swimming,' I said. 'You did promise I wouldn't have to do it, honestly you did.'

Miss Hamer-Cotton sighed. 'I know your mother mentioned that you're worried about swimming. But there's no need to get into such a state. We're not going to let you drown, you know. Uncle Ron isn't going to throw you in the deep end. He'll teach you exactly what to do and you can wear an inflatable ring if it makes you feel safer and—'

'But I won't feel safe, no matter what. Please, I *can't* have swimming lessons.'

'I wish you wouldn't keep interrupting me, dear.

Now, go and get your breakfast and stop worrying about swimming. I'll have a special word with Uncle Ron about you. I know you'll find him very kind and understanding. Do you know he even managed to teach a little blind girl to swim? She was diving about like a little dolphin by the end of her holiday with us.'

'I can't go in the water. My doctor said. It's my heart.'

'You're being silly now, Stella,' said Miss Hamer-Cotton briskly. 'We ask all our parents to sign a form saying that their children are fit and healthy. There's nothing wrong with you. So stop telling silly fibs and go and eat your breakfast before I get cross.'

'I can't go in swimming. I haven't got a swimming costume.'

'I've got some spare ones. No problem. Now run along.'

I thought hard as I walked to the door. Then I turned round.

'Could I see the Brigadier, please?'

Miss Hamer-Cotton shrugged her shoulders so that Tinkypoo slid to the ground. She stood up and put her hands on her hips.

'Why do you want to see the Brigadier?'

'I want to ask him if I have to go in swimming.'

Miss Hamer-Cotton held on to her hips. Her

knuckles went white. 'The Brigadier is much too busy to be bothered with silly little girls like you. Now go away at once or you'll lose a team point.'

'I'm going to write to my mother,' I said. 'It's not fair. You did promise.'

'You're in Emerald, aren't you?' said Miss Hamer-Cotton ominously. 'Right. You have now lost one team point for the Emeralds.'

I slunk out of her room. It wasn't fair. And she hated me now. She'd keep on picking on me the whole time I was here. Maybe she'd even lock me up in the tower like the child crying in the night.

The others hadn't believed me. Even Karen said she thought it might have been a dream, which showed she was completely mental, because how could we both have the same dream?

I paused in the middle of the corridor. I was in enough trouble as it was. And yet I badly wanted to find out where the crying had come from. My feet started creeping down the corridor of their own accord. My trainers squeaked noisily and I glared at them. And then a door opened at the end of the right hand corridor and I heard more footsteps. Shuffly old-ladies-sandals footsteps. It was Orange Overall, only she was wearing a sort of pinafore thing today, with a flowery purple pattern. She was carrying something in an old towel and she scowled when she saw me.

'You're going the wrong way. Downstairs! Go on, go and get your breakfast. Dear oh dear, you kids.'

I hated being called a kid but I wasn't up to any more arguments. I trailed downstairs and found the dining room. I stood hovering in the doorway. I knew there were only about forty children staying at Evergreen but there seemed to be at least four hundred chattering and chomping away. They were sitting at benches around four big tables. One had a lime green tablecloth, one olive, one jade, and one emerald. The cloths were all copiously egg-stained already.

I saw Marzipan waving at me and I ran over to her and sat down beside her with the rest of the Emerald girls. The Emerald boys were opposite. There were only four of them. Three looked about my age, but one was so little he didn't even look old enough to feed himself. Scrambled egg dripped up his plump little arms to his elbows.

'I think I'd better help you,' said Karen.

The little boy shook his head vigorously.

'Don't need help,' he said, and continued spooning haphazardly.

Karen shrugged and helped the little girl with the donkey instead, spreading her toast and cutting it into strips. The little girl sucked at a slither of toast as if it was an iced lolly.

Marzipan had saved me a plate of scrambled eggs, two slices of toast, and a cup of tea. It was kind of her but I wasn't sure I was grateful. The scrambled egg was lukewarm and had set solidly, like a primrose jelly. I tried a mouthful and pulled a disgusted face.

'Are you leaving those eggs?' said the boy sitting opposite me. 'Then give us your dregs.'

He was large. Much larger than Marzipan. He slurped up my scrambled eggs in no time.

'Do you really like them?' I asked, amazed.

'Of course not. This food is absolute pigswill,' he said cheerfully. 'But I'm hungry, aren't I? Brill!'

'Here, do you want the rest of mine, Fatty?' said Karen, passing her plate.

'Who are you calling Fatty, Batty?' said the fat boy, reaching over the table and pretending to punch her. 'See this hand here? Call me that again and I'll shove it straight through your ear.'

'You touch me and I'll tell,' said Karen.

'Tell, smell. Pass your plate, I can't wait. My name's James. I'm a poet and I know it. You think you're it and you make me spit.'

I nudged Marzipan and we both giggled. Karen passed her plate without saying another word. She looked to Louise for support. But Louise

42

wasn't taking any notice of her. She was nibbling daintily at a toast crust, tossing her lovely long hair about and smiling mysteriously. She was being watched by the oldest Emerald boy. He was tall and good looking although his fair hair was so tightly curled it looked as if his mum had given him a home perm. He couldn't take his eyes off Louise, more fool him.

There was one more boy at the table. He had odd sticking up hair almost as short as mine. He was eating his scrambled eggs and reading an old *Beano* comic.

'Can I have a look at that *Beano* after you?' Karen asked.

He ignored her. He didn't seem to be taking any notice of anyone but the Bash Street Kids, but when the little girl with the donkey discarded her sodden strip of toast and slipped down her chair until only her forehead was visible above the table he felt in his pocket and brought out a rather dusty sugar lump. He didn't say anything but he put it beside the donkey's mouth. The little girl didn't say anything either but she made the donkey nibble at the sugar lump and when she thought no one was looking she ate it herself.

The little boy with the scrambled egg up to his elbows looked even more of a baby but he could obviously look after himself. Karen was asking everyone their name. The boy staring so stupidly at Louise was called Richard. The boy with the *Beano* was called Alan.

'And what's your name, little boy?' Karen asked.

'Bilbo,' said the little boy, licking toast crumbs from his mouth.

'Billy?' Karen repeated uncertainly.

'*Bilbo*,' he shouted. 'Wash your ears out.'

'You can't be called Bilbo. That's even dafter than Marzipan,' said Karen.

'It's not daft. It's in a book,' said the little boy.

'What book?'

'I don't know. It's got elves and wizards and things. My dad reads me bits.'

'More flipping fairy stories. Sounds your sort of rubbish, Baldy.'

'It's not rubbish at all,' I said triumphantly. 'He's talking about a book called *The Hobbit* and it's a smashing book, so there. We had it read to us at school. There's a Bilbo in that.'

'Oh yes, I've read that book too,' said Louise.

'See,' I said to Karen.

Then Miss Hamer-Cotton came into the dining room and I stopped feeling so cocky. Had she really meant it about that team point? I slid down a bit on the bench so that she wouldn't notice me.

She clapped her hands, smiling, her teeth as

white and even as the pearls round her neck. I wished she was wearing her silly tracksuit. She looked so much more bossy and frightening in her skirt and blouse and high heels.

'Good morning, everyone,' she said jauntily. She didn't sound cross. 'How are we all this morning, mm? Have you seen the sun shining? It's an absolutely super day. Now, I want everyone down at the pool at ten o'clock. Get into your swimming things first, of course. There are a few spare costumes in the games room just in case anyone has come without swimming gear.' She looked in my direction. 'Then after lunch there'll be a quiet time for writing letters and making out your activity timetables. And at three o'clock there's our hike to Hampton Hill. I hope you're all looking forward to it?'

One or two goody-goodies murmured obediently. I wiggled my eyebrows at Marzipan. Miss Hamer-Cotton noticed and I quickly tried to smooth them back into place.

'Now, I want you to carry your crocks through to the kitchen and wipe down your tables and sweep up any little messy bits on the floor. We must all do our best to help the staff, mustn't we? At the end of the week I shall give a team point to the tidiest table. Which reminds me . . . ' Her sunny smile clouded. It wasn't going to be all

45

right after all. 'Someone has lost a team point already. Stella Stebbings.'

Everyone peered round like loonies. I pretended to peer too so they didn't all know it was me, but it was no use.

'Stand up, Stella,' she commanded.

So I had to. Everyone stared at me. I went horribly hot. I knew I was going red.

'Yes, no wonder you're blushing. Fancy losing a team point already! And for rude behaviour too. It's not very fair on the other Emeralds, is it? So if I were you, Stella, I'd try hard to be very good indeed today. You want to win that team point back again as soon as possible, don't you?'

I wanted to yell no, but I wasn't that stupid. I just stood there until she swept out of the room, then I sat down on the bench with a bump. Louise stood up. She came over to me and thumped me hard in the back.

'You pig!' she said furiously. 'I'm going to get you for that.'

Chapter Five

I stood at the poolside in my borrowed swimming
costume. It was an awful white puckered object
with silly straps that tied at the back of the
neck. I was scared the boys might try to undo
them. But I was far more scared of the swimming
pool.

I'd thought it would be one of those turquoise rectangles, but it was worse. It was a real pool, like a big pond. The water was as brown and bubbly as beer and weed trailed all over the place in long green strands.

'What are all them snakey things?' Janie asked suspiciously. She clutched the child with the donkey. 'We're not going in there, are we? We don't want snakey things nibbling our toes.'

'How can we have races in this squitty little pond? It's just a kiddies' paddling pool,' said Louise, scornfully.

'Yes, and it looks dirty to me,' said Karen. 'They could at least have a proper swimming pool with clean blue water. This place is a real dump.'

'Don't let's go in swimming then,' I said quickly. 'You're right, Karen, it is dirty. Look at the colour. Maybe there aren't any sewers at Evergreen. I think they just empty all the loos into the pool.'

'Yuck! Shut up, Baldy. You are disgusting,' said Karen. She looked at Louise. 'She is joking, isn't she?'

'She's scared,' said Louise hatefully. 'She just wants to get out of swimming. She wants to make trouble and then the Emeralds will lose another team point. Don't let's take any notice of her. She's just a snivelling little coward. In fact I vote we all stop talking to her altogether.'

I felt sick but I stuck my chin in the air.

'Goodie goodie,' I said. 'I'm fed up with your snobby whining drivel anyway.'

I hoped I sounded as if I didn't care. Some of the boys laughed and I was almost sure they were laughing at Louise and not me, so I felt a bit better. But then Uncle Ron finished with all the Jades.

'Come on then, Emeralds. Your turn next. Let's be having you. Into the pool—and use the steps, OK?'

Alan wasn't listening. He leapt up into the air like Superman. He tucked himself into a ball, whizzed round, and then shot out straight again and entered the pool with scarcely a ripple. We all stared at him when he surfaced, shaking the water out of his hair. Even Louise looked impressed. But Uncle Ron was furious.

'I told you to use the steps, didn't you hear me?'

'Sorry,' said Alan, smiling. 'I always dive in. Force of habit. I just forgot.'

'Nonsense! You just wanted to show-off,' Uncle Ron thundered. 'Nobody but a fool dives into a strange pool like that. What if it was only a couple of feet deep? You'd have broken your neck, lad.'

'I saw the other kids swimming,' Alan argued, red in the face. 'I knew how deep it was.'

'Watch me! *Watch!*' little Bilbo shouted from the steps.

He tried to copy Alan, leaping like a little pink frog. He didn't have time to tuck up but he did manage to bend forward. He hit the water with such a splatter that we were all soaked. Uncle Ron threw himself after him but Bilbo bobbed up again immediately.

'I did it, didn't I?' he spluttered. 'I dived just like Alan. Did you see? Wasn't I clever? I dived, didn't I, I dived.'

'See what I mean?' Uncle Ron roared at Alan, picking Bilbo up and struggling with him to the shallows by the steps. 'Think you're so clever, don't you? But these little kids will follow your fat-headed example and drown themselves.'

'I won't drown. I can swim. Nearly,' said Bilbo. 'And I can dive now too, can't I? Did you see me dive? Wow, I can dive! I can dive just as good as you, can't I, Alan?'

Alan didn't reply. He was even redder. I felt all squirmy and sorry for him. Uncle Ron was smirking. I hated him, even though I knew he was right.

'Come on, you ladies at the edge of the pool. Get in the water and get your pretty cossies wet,' said Uncle Ron. He blew his nose noisily in the water with his hand. 'Come *on*. All of you, in the pool and stand in line. Then one by one swim up to the first marker. Those of you who are good swimmers go as far as the second marker.

But none of you go any further, even if you've been entered in the next Olympics. Understood, laddie?'

Alan nodded. I waited, praying. Louise slid daintily into the water, sucking in her stomach to show off her pink and white bikini properly. She'd plaited her famous hair and coiled it up on top of her head so that it looked like a little crown. She was fairer than me but she had a lovely even tan. I couldn't stand Louise.

Karen looked very white and pimply beside her. She got into the water gingerly, shrieking as it lapped at her legs. Janie shrieked too. She held out her hand to the child with the donkey.

'Come on in, I'll look after you,' she called.

The child hesitated, then laid the donkey in the grass, covered him up with a towel until only his muzzle peeped out, and crept down the steps.

I prayed harder.

'It's not very deep, Stella, honestly,' Marzipan whispered. 'It'll only come up to your waist.'

She took hold of me awkwardly by the wrist. She was just trying to be friendly but I was scared she might pull me in, so I snatched my arm away.

'No. Leave go of me,' I muttered fiercely.

So Marzipan wobbled down the steps into the water. Her swimming costume was much too tight. The water came up to her thighs and she shifted uncomfortably as it rippled against her. She kept tugging at her costume at the back to try to make it cover more of her. The boys started making fun of her and sniggering. Marzipan pretended not to hear but I wasn't very good at ignoring people.

'Shut up, you lot. Take a look in the mirror if you want to see a really funny sight.'

They just laughed and splashed me. Uncle Ron swam to the steps and bounded up to them. He stood beside me, dripping. Even when they were wet the ginger hairs on his chest were as thick and bristly as a doormat.

'Stop mucking about, you lot. No splashing,' he said. Then he bent his head down to my level. 'I hear you're not too fond of swimming, Stella. Not to worry. Bend down and put your hand in the pool. It's a bit cold at first but you'll warm up once you get in properly.'

He went on making encouraging noises but I was too scared to listen. He was dripping on my bare toes, making me shiver. I felt so sick. That suddenly seemed the answer to my prayers. I jerked my tummy in and out, heaved, and thought very hard about the scrambled eggs I'd had at breakfast. I imagined them shooting into the water, lapping against Louise.

'Come on, pet. One step at a time.' Uncle Ron

put his hand on my shoulder. The hand that had blown his nose.

'I'm going to be sick,' I whispered.

He peered at me.

'All right then. You do look a bit green. You'd better trot back to the house,' he said, wonderfully, unbelievably.

'Uncle Ron's daft. She's not feeling sick at all. She just wants to get out of swimming,' said Louise.

Uncle Ron peered at me again.

'Hang on. Maybe you'd be better getting into the pool now, getting it over and done with. Come on.'

His grip tightened. I was so scared he might throw me in that I rushed forward and slithered down the steps, losing my balance and falling into the frothy water. I didn't go right under but I thought I might. I screamed and everyone laughed.

I stood there, shivering, while everyone swam. Alan was easily the best swimmer. Bilbo couldn't swim at all. He splashed and struggled but couldn't get anywhere. He was put in the beginners class. So was Janie. She could swim a little but she kept fussing about the water weed and shrieking and spluttering and going under. The child with the donkey surprised everyone by swimming a neat little breaststroke to the first marker and back again. Then she sat on the steps, looking longingly at her donkey in his towel. Louise was the second best swimmer after Alan, Karen got to the second marker, even Marzipan managed it although it made her puff and blow a bit.

But I just stood there uselessly.

'Have a go, Stella. It's all right, I'll hold you up, I promise,' said Uncle Ron.

I shook my head but he persisted. I had to kick with my feet while he held his hand under my chin. I couldn't do it.

'Come on, pet, try. Kick!'

I wanted to kick him, kick Louise, kick them all. I ended up in the baby's beginner class with Janie and Bilbo.

We had to sit at the edge of the pool while the intermediate and advanced swimmers took it in turns to dive off the rickety old springboard.

'It's not fair. I can dive. Why won't they let me dive? You all saw me dive. It's not fair,' Bilbo chuntered continuously.

Janie played with her plaits and waved at the child in the water.

I sat and shivered and sulked, but I watched when it was Alan's turn to dive. He ran along the springy plank and stood at the end, up on his toes, ready to take off. And then Uncle Ron put his foot on the board and gave it a quick shove. Alan lost his balance and fell. He tucked in his legs but he didn't have time to twist and turn properly and he crashed into the water as clumsily as Bilbo.

Uncle Ron tutted. 'Not quite good enough. We'll put you in the Intermediates for diving.'

Alan shook his head violently, spray flying everywhere.

'That's not fair! I lost my balance, it wasn't a proper dive.'

'Sorry,' said Uncle Ron. 'We'll put you down as Intermediate for this week. You can try again for the Advanced group next Sunday.'

Alan did a duck-dive but he wasn't quick enough. I saw his tears of rage. Louise saw too.

'Little cry-baby! Just because he didn't get chosen for the Advanced group,' she sneered.

Louise had been chosen. Of course.

We were supposed to drip back to the dormis to get changed. There were no changing facilities at the pool apart from one little bamboo hut without windows. Uncle Ron went inside, whistling. Alan pulled a hideous face at his back. I went over to him.

'Clear off,' he mumbled, scrubbing at his face with his fist.

'He wobbled the board with his foot. I'm sure he did it deliberately,' I said.

55

'I thought he did. The pig,' said Alan.

'He is,' I agreed.

We started making pig noises. They got louder and snortier. Uncle Ron started whistling inside the little hut. Alan and I stopped snorting and spluttered.

'Do you think he heard?' I whispered.

Alan shook his head and stared at the hut.

'I wish there was a chair or something we could shove against the door,' he hissed. 'Wouldn't it be great if he couldn't get out?'

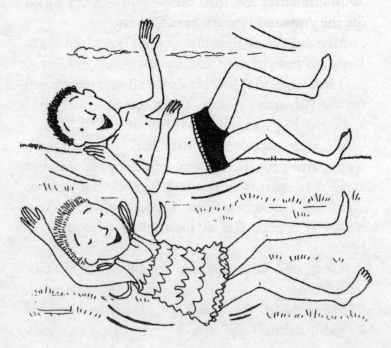

'Not half! We could keep him a prisoner. We could slop scrambled eggs through the chinks in the bamboo and he'd have to lick them up to stay alive,' I giggled.

The chinks in the bamboo gave me a sudden glorious idea. I whispered to Alan. We crept right up to the hut. Uncle Ron whistled merrily inside as he got changed. Alan and I held our breath. We screwed up our eyes and peered through the chinks. We had a good long look and then I started spluttering. Alan did too. We started running. We ran until we were safe in the wood and then we fell on the grass and whooped with laughter.

Chapter Six

Marzipan was waiting for me when I got back to the house.

'Where have you been?' she asked plaintively.

I felt a bit guilty. 'Sorry. I was just mucking about with Alan. I've got some chocolate in my drawer, do you want a bit? I'm starving, aren't you?'

But when we got upstairs to the Emerald dormi we found someone had been at my chocolate already. There was a great bite out of it. All my bedclothes were in a heap on the floor and my clothes were strewn around the room. I found a note pinned to Squeakycheese's remaining paw.

'TIDY UP, BALDY, OR YOU'LL LOSE ANOTHER TEAM POINT.'

'The pigs, the pigs, the pigs!' I shouted.

There was no sign of Louise and Karen. Janie and the child with the donkey looked worried. The child held her donkey in front of her like a shield.

'My things, all my things!' I raged, rushing round trying to gather them all up. 'My fairytale book, look, just flung on the floor. If any of the pages have got torn I'll kill them. And my notebook— and they've even got at my fruit gums! Look, all over the floor, all in the dust. Well, I'll show them all right. I'll *show* them.'

I ran to Karen's bed first and ripped back the covers.

'Don't! Oh, Stella, please don't,' said Marzipan, catching hold of me. 'If you muck up their things then they'll just do it again to you and it'll go on and on.'

'I'm not going to let those two pigs get away with it,' I said furiously, my fists clenched.

'That's what they want. Don't you see that? And if you do something to them I bet Karen tells and then you'll be the one to get into trouble,' said Marzipan. 'Leave her things, Stella. Don't stoop to their level. Come on, I'll make your bed for you. You two, help Stella put all her things back.'

Janie helped as hard as she could, even dusting things with her damp towel. The child with the donkey carried him around with her so her arms were full already but she managed to collect the bitten bar of chocolate. She held it out to me.

'Thanks. The cheek! Noshing away at my

chocolate like that. Well, we might as well finish it now, eh?'

I shared it out between us. I crammed a few extra squares into my mouth when I hoped no one was watching. After all, it was my chocolate.

It was just as well we'd eaten it because lunch was a bitter disappointment. I wouldn't really call a very small hot dog, half a tomato, and ten crisps *lunch*, it was more a snack. There was trifle for pudding but that wasn't very exciting either, and the yellow custard looked suspiciously like the scrambled eggs at breakfast.

'This is not a hot dog,' I said, munching the tepid pink meat. 'This is a lukewarm puppy.'

Alan looked up from his *Beano* and grinned.

'Hark at Baldy. She thinks that's funny,' Karen hissed furiously.

She was obviously annoyed because I hadn't even mentioned the vandalized dormi. She and Louise had been all red in the face, trying to act nonchalantly, when I'd come down to the dining room. I'd taken no notice of them whatsoever.

Louise was taking no notice of Karen now. She was swapping crisps with Richard and acting idiotically. Karen kept trying to talk to her.

'Do stop butting in, Karen,' Louise said irritably.

Karen sighed. She fiddled with her lunch. She leant back in her chair, rocking on two legs. The chair tipped. She rocked harder. The chair tipped further and then slipped and Karen fell backwards with a shriek.

We all stood up and stared at her. Miss Hamer-Cotton came flying across the room, looking terrified. Karen lay very still, her legs sticking up stiffly.

'I think she's dead,' Janie whispered, awed.

'Don't be silly,' said Miss Hamer-Cotton, feeling Karen all over for broken bones. 'You poor old thing, did you hit your head?'

'I'm not sure,' Karen mumbled, sounding shaken.

Miss Hamer-Cotton helped her to her feet.

'You really were asking for trouble, you know. You mustn't tip your chair like that. How do you feel now?'

'A bit funny,' said Karen.

'Come on, I'll take you upstairs. You'd better have a lie down for a little while,' said Miss Hamer-Cotton.

So Karen missed out on half her hot dog and all her trifle.

'She's to blame. Still, it's a shame,' said James, reaching for her plate.

'I wouldn't worry too much about Karen,' I said, still feeling cross. 'She's full up already. With chocolate. *My* chocolate. Eh, Louise?'

Louise smiled serenely and accepted another crisp

from Richard. She didn't seem very concerned about Karen either.

When we went up to the dormi after lunch Karen wasn't lying down after all. She was parading around in Louise's white jeans and red and white shirt.

'Get them off at once!' Louise said, outraged. 'I didn't say you could try them on, did I?'

'I'm sorry, Louise. I didn't think you'd mind, seeing as we're best friends.'

'Well, I do mind. And I'm not even sure I want to be best friends any more,' said Louise.

Karen looked stricken. She folded Louise's clothes with elaborate care and offered to lend Louise her new turquoise felt tip pen when we had to write letters home.

'No thanks. I don't want to use your mucky old felt tip,' said Louise, flashing her posh Harley pen.

Karen sniffled as she wrote her letter. She kept looking at me. I was sure she was writing horrid things about me to her mother.

My own letter took me ages. Mum had given me some special airmail letters already addressed to these foreign hotels. By the time I'd written all about the swimming lessons and how unfair it was and how I hated Uncle Ron and Miss Hamer-Cotton I'd used up nearly all the room. So I just added, 'I have a friend called Marzipan (funny name but she's nice) and one of the boys isn't bad but Karen and Louise are *pigs* and they ate my chocolate, Love from Stella.'

Miss Hamer-Cotton collected our letters for posting and handed out activity sheets.

'Fill them up carefully, girls, in your neatest writing. How are you feeling, Karen? You've got your colour back now. I think you'll be fit for the hike. We're meeting downstairs in the hall at half past two. Wear your comfiest shoes, it's quite a walk to Hampton Hill.'

'Do we have to go, Miss?' asked Janie. 'I don't like long walks. They're boring. Me and my friend would sooner play here in the bedroom.'

Miss Hamer-Cotton smiled stupidly as if Janie was joking and didn't even bother to answer her.

I concentrated on my activity sheet. I didn't want to do judo or climbing or five-a-side football or rounders or rambling or mime or music. I didn't want to BMX bike or box. I didn't want to play chess or computer games. I didn't know what macramé was but I was sure I didn't want to do it. I certainly didn't want to swim. About all that was left was Art. I didn't mind doing Art so I put Art again and again, morning and afternoon, on Monday, Tuesday, Wednesday, Thursday, and Friday.

'You can't do that,' said Marzipan. 'It says so on the back of the paper, look. You have to do four different activities each day. And you've got to fit in two swimming sessions a week as well.'

'I'll make out I haven't read the back of the paper,' I said quickly.

I felt a bit worried when I handed my activity sheet to Miss Hamer-Cotton but she was too busy getting us all organized for the hike to notice. She kept saying it was going to be such fun—but she didn't actually go on the hike herself, I noticed. I bet she put her feet up all afternoon and watched the telly.

Uncle Ron was in charge. He was in his ghastly grey tracksuit again, with a large orange haversack bobbing up and down on his back. He had a whole load of student Uncles and Aunties to help keep an eye on us. They were mostly sad and spotty and had silly names like Jimbo and Jilly. They ushered us through the woods, past the dreaded swimming pool, and along by the stream and across the meadows towards the dismally distant brown hummock of Hampton Hill.

I lagged behind with Marzipan. Alan walked with us, whipping at the bushes with a long snappy stick. It made a wonderful swishing sound. Marzipan jumped every time he did it.

'Let me have a go with your stick, Alan, please,' I begged.

I kept on at him until he gave in and handed it over.

'Right, start cowering, everyone,' I said, snapping the stick. 'This is when I start to get my own back. Do you hear me, Karen-Copycat and Louise Lavatory? Lash lash lash. And you can watch out too, Uncle Pong, if you try and get me in that pool again it'll be lash lash lash for you too.'

'Stella, mind. You very nearly cut me. And keep your voice down, he'll hear,' Marzipan whispered.

'I'm not scared of him, not now I'm armed,' I said, lashing.

I lashed a bit too loudly and Uncle Ron noticed.

'Hey you, Stella! Watch what you're doing, for goodness sake. You'll have someone's eye out if you're not careful.' He came jogging up, seized the stick, and snapped it into matchsticks.

'Charming,' Alan muttered.

I looked at him guiltily.

'Let's have a song to help us on our way,' Uncle Ron shouted so that everyone could hear. 'How about "Ten Green Bottles"?'

I can't stand that song. I don't see why on earth anyone would want to hang those silly green bottles on a wall. I didn't join in. Marzipan and Alan didn't either. When there was only one green bottle left Uncle Ron and the Jimbos and Jillys were the only ones left singing.

'Come on, you lot, you can do better than that,' Uncle Ron complained. 'I know, we'll divide you up into your teams.'

He taught us this special Evergreen team song. It was even sillier than 'Ten Green Bottles'.

'Jade, Emerald, Olive, and Lime
We are the teams that tick to time.
Lime, Olive, Emerald, and Jade
We are the teams that can't be swayed.
So which of the greens is the best team out?
Open your mouths and let's hear you SHOUT.'

And then the Limes yelled Lime. The Olives yelled Olive. The Jades yelled Jade. And we were supposed to yell Emerald. Only I didn't. And Alan didn't either. Marzipan pretended, opening her mouth wide, but she didn't make any noise.

Then Uncle Ron organized a team singing contest. The Emeralds were set against the Jades. We had to sing 'Half a Pound of Tuppenny Rice' and they had to sing 'Jingle Bells' and we had to see which tune won. Alan and I decided to sing our own song instead. We sang 'We Are The Champions' very loudly indeed. 'We Are The Champions' won and Uncle Ron got cross.

Louise and Karen and some of the other Emeralds

weren't just cross with us, they were furious. They hung back until Uncle Ron and the Jimbos and Jillys and the other children were in the woods at the bottom of Hampton Hill and then there was a fight. There was a lot of pushing and shoving. The child with the donkey got in the way by mistake and was knocked over.

'Watch out! You've hurt my friend!' Janie shouted.

We stopped fighting and stared at the child with the donkey. She got up slowly, rubbing herself.

'She's OK,' said Richard, and seized Alan in a hammerlock.

The little girl stood very still, her face crumpling. She was looking at her donkey. He had been knocked out of her arms. He'd fallen into a huge cowpat. The little girl stared. The donkey stared miserably back, his glass eyes smeared, his soft furry coat dark with dung.

Chapter Seven

'Her donkey!' Janie yelled. 'It's gone in all the cow's thingy, look!'

We all stared. The child without her donkey stuck out her arm desperately. Karen caught hold of her.

'No, don't! It's *covered*. You can't.'

The child started crying. She didn't make a sound. Tears just gathered in her eyes and then spilled silently.

'It'll be all germy now. And it smells,' Janie said, putting her arm round her. 'It can't be helped. Tell you what. I'll let you share my blue teddy.'

'Come on. We'll get into trouble. The others have been out of sight for ages,' said Louise. 'Pull her along, Janie, she'll come with you.'

But she wouldn't. She stood beside the cowpat, trembling.

'Come on, little girl. Come with us,' said Karen, trying to help Janie.

The child ducked away from both of them, crying harder when Karen clung.

'Leave her, Karen, you're just making her worse,' I said.

'You can shut up for a start, Baldy. It was all your fault anyway. If you and Alan hadn't mucked about singing "We Are The Champions" then none of this would have happened. It was Alan who knocked her over, I saw,' said Karen.

I think she was only guessing, but Alan went red. He looked at the child guiltily. His face screwed up.

'Oh my giddy Aunt,' said Alan. 'Don't cry like that. I'll get your silly old donkey.'

He flexed his bare arm, bent down beside the cowpat and reached into it. He groaned as his fingers sank into the smelly mound but he caught hold of the donkey and pulled it free. His arm was bright brown. We all squealed and shuddered and the boys laughed. The child stared, still crying.

'Try wiping it on the grass,' I said.

Alan wiped and wiped. The worst of the sludge came off his arm but the donkey got even dirtier, grass and burrs clinging to his filthy fur.

'Throw it away,' said Louise. 'Pooh, it stinks. You stink too, Alan. Come on, let's catch up the others.'

She rounded everyone up, even Janie.

'We've got to go or we'll get left behind,' Janie said, and she was nearly crying too. 'Leave the donkey. Look, I'll *give* you my blue teddy, I won't even have a share in him, OK? Come on.'

The child hung back, staring at the donkey. Alan had dropped it on the ground and was rubbing at his arm with a dock leaf.

'I can't wait to have a wash,' he said, holding his arm away from him. He looked at the little girl. 'I'm sorry, I can't get it off him. We'll have to dump poor old donkey.'

The child stared. I just couldn't bear the way she was looking. I had to do something.

'I'll make your old donkey better again, you wait and see,' I said. I took hold of him by one smelly old leg and started running back across the meadow.

'Stella! Stella, you're going the wrong way. Stella, come back,' Marzipan shouted.

Someone else was shouting too. It was coming from the woods. It was Uncle Ron and he sounded angry.

I stopped and looked over my shoulder.

'Oh help,' said Karen.

'Come on,' said Louise, running towards the woods.

Karen and Richard and James and Bilbo started running too. Janie hung back, pleading with the child, but Karen came after her and pulled her away.

Marzipan called me again but I shook my head and went on running. I listened though and after a bit I heard people running after me. I grinned.

They caught me up right back by the stream, Marzipan and Alan and the little child.

'What are you playing at, Stella? We're going to get into awful trouble,' Marzipan moaned.

I was too busy to take much notice. I was clinging to a large tuft of grass with one hand and dangling the donkey into the stream with the other. It was horribly cold and uncomfortable and

I was scared I'd slip right in and drown. It was almost as bad as the swimming pool but it couldn't be helped. I had to wash all the muck off the donkey. My arm ached and went numb with cold but I went on swooshing him through the water. The child watched as he bucked and reared and galloped. She'd stopped crying.

'Here, I'll have a go,' said Marzipan.

She was better at sluicing and squeezing. She kept holding the donkey up for inspection and he got cleaner and cleaner each time. When the water trickling from him was crystal clear she squeezed him out thoroughly. The child gasped as she twisted the donkey round and round.

'It's all right, I'm not hurting him,' said Marzipan. 'Here he is, then.'

She handed him over. The child sat on the bank and cradled the donkey. She wiped his eyes with the hem of her dress, she smelt him, she fingered his fur—and then she hugged him.

'Careful, he's still sopping wet,' said Marzipan.

The child didn't care. She hugged him tightly to her chest, rocking backwards and forwards.

'It was my idea to wash him in the stream,' I reminded her.

She smiled at me.

'I think he liked his swim,' I said. 'What's his name then?'

The little girl looked at me, her head on one side.

'I know. It's Eeyore,' I said.

'No, it's not,' said the little girl.

She spoke! She actually spoke, in a dear little squeaky-mouse voice. I nodded triumphantly at Marzipan and Alan. *I'd* got her to speak.

'What is his name then?' I asked.

'My donkey's a she, not a he. She's called Dora Donkey.'

'Dora!' I struggled not to laugh. 'Hello, Dora Donkey.' I shook the donkey's sodden hoof. 'How are you today then, Dora? Would you like a cup of carrot juice, eh?'

I pretended to give her one. The child giggled, especially when I made Dora drink with great slurps.

'And what's your name?' I asked.

She shook her head.

'I'll guess. It ought to be something to go with Dora. Let's see. Cora? Flora? Leonora?'

The child spluttered with laughter.

'It's Rosemary,' she announced.

'That's a pretty name,' I said. 'There's a girl at my school called Mary Rose, that's Rosemary backwards, and everyone used to chant this daft rhyme "Mary Rose sat on a pin, Mary Rose" until Mary Rose got really mad so I suggested she should get her own back and bring some pins to school and—'

'Trust you!' said Marzipan. 'Come on then, Stella.'

'Come on where?'

'Don't be daft! We've got to catch the others up. And we aren't half going to get into awful trouble too,' said Marzipan, sighing.

I didn't want to think about it and spoil everything. I liked it here, just Marzipan, Rosemary, Alan, and me. I didn't see why we couldn't stay here for a bit longer.

'Don't be an old spoilsport, Marzipan. Let's stop here.' I stretched out on the grass. 'Here Rosemary, pass Dora to me. We'll spread her out in the sun and get her tummy dry, eh? And while she's sunbathing we could make her a daisychain. She'd like that, wouldn't she?'

Rosemary nodded. I loved the way she looked at me now, as if I were a queen and she my little serving maid.

'When I've made Dora a daisychain I'll make one for you, Stella, a really long special one, because you made Dora better again,' said Rosemary.

'Cheek! *I* was the one who got your donkey out of the smelly old cowpat,' said Alan, but he didn't really mind.

He rolled up his jeans and went in paddling, wincing a bit at the icy water.

'Oh dear, does Little Precious want a special daisy necklace too then?' I teased.

Alan splashed water at me but I ducked behind Marzipan.

'Do stop mucking about, you two,' she said crossly, dabbing at herself. 'Please let's go and find the others.'

'I'm staying here,' I said. 'I don't want to go on a boring hike with Uncle Pong.'

Alan fell about laughing. 'Uncle Pong. How perfect.' He staggered about and nearly tripped on a rock. He bent and tugged at it. 'It's ever so narrow here. I bet we could make a dam. Come and help, Stella.'

'No fear. I'm not going in that freezing old stream. Get Marzipan to help. Go on, Marz, show us your muscles,' I said, starting to thread daisies.

Marzipan chewed at her lip worriedly, realizing we really were staying.

'Do you want one of my fruit gums?' I said quickly, searching my pockets. 'They're not really that fluffy, and we can always wash them. You can have the strawberry one if you like, Marzipan.'

Marzipan sucked the strawberry and made a daisychain but she didn't look happy.

'I'll be the one they'll blame, because I'm the oldest,' she said. 'What do you think they'll do to us?'

'Nothing. They'll just make us lose a silly old team point. Who cares?' I said.

'They might . . . ' Marzipan tugged at the grass miserably, trying to decide what they really might do to us. But she wasn't very good at making up Dire Consequences. It was a game I loved.

'They might put us in that big tower,' I said. 'Yes, they could lock us up in it.' I remembered the Princess Stellarina story I'd started in my new notebook and I started telling it. I was just doing it to tease poor old Marzipan at first but then I got carried away. I went on with the story and they all listened, even Alan. I'd have been mad to have stopped with an audience like that, so I went on and on until my voice started to go croaky.

I was right in the middle of the story. Princess Stellarina was being smothered with one of Uncle Pong's disgusting tracksuits. She was fainting with the fumes but Prince Alaghad couldn't rescue her because he was tied up in the dungeon with several ropes of Hag Hateful-Catty's pearls and the melancholy maiden Marzine had wandered into the marshes by moonlight and had been captured by the evil Lavatrise and Kopy Karen and Little Red Rosy Posy had gone galloping after her on her noble steed Interflora but she had fallen in a filthy mire and they were both being sucked to a dreadful death.

I wasn't sure how to sort them all out. I paused and then flopped on to my back.

'End of part one. Will Princess Stellarina be able to endure her ordeal? Will Prince Alaghad burst his pearl chains? Will melancholy Marzine escape the demon duo Lavatrise and Kopy Karen? Will little Red Rosy Posy be dragged from the quickdung in time? Listen out for the next instalment of the Ever Exciting Adventures at Everblack.' I did a dramatic Tra-la-la-laa. There was a long silence.

'Were you making it all up?' said Marzipan.

'Of course!'

'I mean, you didn't get it out of a book?'

'How could I?' I said.

I tried to sound casual but I wanted to jump around and show off I was so pleased they were impressed by my story.

'Stellarina and Alaghad! You're even more of a nutcase than I thought,' said Alan.

I wasn't sure, but I think he was impressed too.

'Tell some more,' Rosemary begged.

But I couldn't think of any more for the moment so we made some more daisychains instead and Alan built a dam. The daisychains kept breaking and the dam leaked but it didn't really matter.

No one had a watch so we weren't really sure about the time. We'd long since finished up the fruit gums and were starting to get ravenous.

Marzipan didn't think it could be more than four o'clock but the rest of us began to wonder if we'd missed tea. Perhaps I hadn't been quite so clever after all.

Then I heard the faint but familiar strains of ten green bottles oh-so-gently falling.

'They're coming back! Quick, let's hide,' I hissed, and we all crawled into the middle of a big bush. The singing got louder and louder and then we could actually see feet tramping along beside the stream. I spotted huge great trainers and grey tracksuit legs and nudged Alan. He nudged me back and we got the giggles and nearly choked.

'Shut up, shut up,' Marzipan mouthed desperately.

'It's all right. They're making too much racket,' I whispered.

The feet were petering out now. I peered through the leaves and saw the rest of the Emeralds looking very hot and cross and bored.

'I bet nobody even noticed we were missing,' I said.

I thought a bit.

'So let's tag on the end with the others now,' I suggested. 'And then no one will be any the wiser.'

The Emeralds were, of course. Janie fell on Rosemary and Dora and hugged them with all her heart. Louise and Karen weren't in a hugging mood.

'Where have you been?' Louise demanded furiously. 'Uncle Ron counted us all when we got to Hampton Hill and Karen and the boys and I had to keep bobbing about to get counted twice or the Emeralds would have lost another flipping team point. What have you been *doing*?'

We smiled at her and wouldn't tell.

Chapter Eight

Rosemary couldn't stop talking now that she'd found her voice. She talked all evening and she was still squeaking away long after Miss Hamer-Cotton had switched out the light in our dormi.

'I'm ever so tired, Rosemary. Couldn't we go to sleep now?' Janie begged.

'I'm not a bit tired,' said Rosemary.

'Well I am,' Louise groaned. 'Put your wretched donkey over your head and pipe down.'

Rosemary did as she was told.

'Dora smells funny,' she said, sounding smothered.

Karen snorted. 'Of course she does, stupid. She's been in a cowpat, yuck yuck yuck. You shouldn't put it round your face, you'll catch some awful disease.'

'No I won't. Will I, Stella?'

For some reason Rosemary kept asking me things now. It was beginning to annoy the others.

'Stella washed all the cow stuff away so Dora doesn't smell nasty any more,' Rosemary continued.

'She just smells funny. Wet. Like my swimming costume when it's been rolled up in my towel a long time.'

'Is she still wet then?' said Marzipan. 'You'd better not have her in bed with you.'

'But I can't sleep without her.'

'You don't seem to be able to sleep with her either,' said Louise.

'I can't help it. I said, I'm just not tired,' said Rosemary, tossing to and fro. 'And I can't get comfy. My sheets are all wrinkled up and my pillow won't go right and Dora can't get comfy either.'

'Shall I tuck you up?' said Karen, getting out of bed. 'Oh for goodness sake, your donkey's still sopping. No wonder you can't get comfy. Look, put it over here and—'

'No! I want Dora!'

'You can't, you'll get pneumonia. And I bet it's still crawling with germs. You'll end up with foot and mouth disease if you don't watch out.'

'Give me Dora!' Rosemary roared.

'Give her it back, Karen, or she'll wake the whole house,' said Louise impatiently.

Karen flung Dora back to Rosemary.

'Stella, can you get me comfy?' Rosemary called.

Karen said something very rude indeed. I got out of bed and went over to Rosemary.

'OK then, let's get you sorted out. Let me have a little chat with my friend Dora. Oh, I see. She says she wants her own bed tonight so she can stretch her hooves and swish her tail about. Here we are, this can be her pillow and this can be her coverlet.'

'Do you mind? That's my cardigan. Get it off that smelly germy old donkey,' Karen shouted.

'Will you shut up, Karen?' Louise demanded. 'You've got a voice like a foghorn. Just get into bed and stop interfering.'

Karen snatched her cardigan and slunk back to bed. I didn't even glance at her but I knew she was looking daggers at me. I rearranged Dora's bed and tucked her up and then I tucked Rosemary up too.

'Now go to sleep like good girls,' I said, patting Dora's matted mane and Rosemary's curls.

'We want a story,' said Rosemary. 'Please, Stella. Tell us a story. Tell about Princess Stellarina.'

'Princess Stellarina!' Karen snorted. 'How incredibly yucky can you get? Princess Stellarina, did you ever!'

'Princess Stellarina is private,' I said quickly to Rosemary. 'But I'll read you a fairy story out of my book if you like. It's a hundred years old, my book, and it's got lovely coloured pictures. It's ever so valuable.'

Rosemary sat up in bed and switched on her torch so that I'd be able to see to read. I went to my locker to get the fairy tale book, wondering which story to choose. Not a very long one, I was too tired. Rosemary would like a story with a donkey in it but the one in my book was a bit silly, all about a hen and a dog who kept climbing on the donkey's back. I decided to read one of my own favourites, Snow White or Cinderella.

I found my book and as I picked it up the blue leather spine came away in my hand. The front of the book flapped loose and the back was all tearing away too. My book was falling to pieces. My precious valuable book.

'Stella,' Rosemary called. 'Stella, what are you doing? Can't you find your book?'

I couldn't even speak. Let it be a mistake, I muttered to myself. Let it be all right after all. Let it be some sort of trick.

I went and switched on the light so that I could see properly. It was even worse than I'd thought. My book was ruined.

'Have you gone mad, Stella?' said Louise, blinking in the sudden brightness. 'Switch that light off at once or Miss Hamer-Cotton will be along.'

'Look at my book,' I croaked, holding out the blue leather tatters.

There was a small silence.

'What's happened to it, Stella?' Rosemary whispered.

'I'll tell you what's happened,' I said. 'I'll *tell* you. Someone's torn it. Someone's taken hold of it and ripped and ripped until they pulled it all to bits.'

'But who—?'

'I'll tell you who,' I shrieked and I ran over to Karen. 'You did it, didn't you? You ripped up my book.'

'I didn't! Don't be mad. I never touched your stupid book,' Karen gabbled. 'Louise, we never touched her book, did we?'

But Louise was staring at Karen, looking shocked. *She* knew Karen had done it too.

'I'll get you for this,' I shouted and I sprang on Karen. I hit her and I pulled her hair hard but then Marzipan and Louise got hold of me and prised me away.

'She's mad, she nearly killed me,' Karen whimpered. 'And I never touched her stupid old book. My lip! I'm sure it's bleeding. And my hair, she was tugging out handfuls. I'm telling on you, Baldy, you wait and see. In the morning I'm going to go straight to Miss Hamer-Cotton.'

'So am I. I'm going to show her my book,' I said, picking it up and trying to fit it together again. 'Criminal damage. That's what it's called.

Criminal damage. This book was worth a fortune. My mum paid twenty—no, fifty pounds for it, and that was years and years ago. It could be worth a hundred pounds now. Maybe even five hundred. You wait, Karen, you're going to end up in prison, you'll see.'

Karen clutched hold of Louise.

'I didn't, did I, Louise? All right, I tipped out some of her clothes, we both did, and we ate a bit of her chocolate, but that's all. It was only a joke. The book might have got tipped on the floor but we didn't rip it, did we?'

'*I* didn't rip it,' said Louise, pushing Karen away.

'But I didn't either! I didn't, I didn't!'

'No, you didn't, Karen,' said Janie.

We all stared at her.

'Me and Rosemary were here when you and Louise mucked up Stella's things. You didn't rip her book.'

'There. See!' said Karen, nodding at me triumphantly. 'Now just say you're sorry, Baldy.'

'She can't have done it, Stella,' said Marzipan. 'I helped you pick up your things and we put the book back and it was fine then, wasn't it?'

I couldn't work it out. I *knew* Karen must have done it somehow. I held on to my book, trying hard not to cry.

'Let me have a look at it,' said Marzipan. 'It's badly torn but it's only the actual outside part. The pages are all right, all the colour plates and everything, look.'

I couldn't bear to look any more.

'It's ruined,' I said flatly, and I took my book and clutched it to my chest.

What was Mum going to say?

'She's crying,' Karen sneered. 'What a baby. All this fuss about a stupid old book. She leaps on me and practically murders me and then doesn't even bother to apologize when it's proved that I didn't do anything to her rotten old book.'

'Yes you did!' I suddenly shrieked. 'And I know when you did it too. When you were up here after lunch, after you'd fallen off your chair. You were here all by yourself. That's when you did it. That's when you ripped up my book.'

Karen shook her head violently.

'No, I didn't. I didn't, I swear I didn't,' she said, but she was wasting her time.

No one believed her, not even Louise. She was a hateful wicked criminal and we all knew it.

'Honestly, Karen,' said Louise. 'Don't you know the difference between a joke and a crime?'

That night the crying was much louder. It was inside our dormi. It was Karen.

Her face was all sore and swollen in the morning.

She'd run out of tissues and kept scrubbing at her face with a sodden wad of lavatory paper. None of us spoke to her, not even Louise.

'Shall I lend her a hankie?' Marzipan whispered to me.

'No! Not after what she's done,' I said, fingering my poor book.

It looked even worse in the daylight.

'Perhaps you could try a bit of sellotape?' said Marzipan.

'You can't just shove sellotape on a book like this.'

'I know, it's the binding that's precious,' said Louise surprisingly. 'My father collects old books. He's always going round antique markets and places like that. If you want I could write to him and ask him to look for another copy of that book for you.'

'Yes, but I haven't the money.'

'Well, you can't really expect my father to pay for it, can you?' said Louise. She paused. 'Are you going to tell Miss Hamer-Cotton?'

Karen sniffled in the corner. A bit of me wanted to make her sniffle even more. But I wasn't a tell-tale.

I didn't even tell Orange Overall/Purple Pinafore. She found the bits of my book when she was tidying up our dormi and she came and found me.

'I want a word with you, Stella,' she said.

Today she was wearing a navy dress with white spots that made my eyes ache.

'It's about your poor story book,' said Dotty Dress.

My heart started thudding and I felt sick. I was sure I was going to get into trouble.

'I don't know how it happened,' I said quickly, terrified that she'd make me go to Miss Hamer-Cotton.

'Never mind how it happened, pet,' she said. She sounded as bothered about it as I was. 'Let's just try to get it mended. I know someone who might be able to sort it out. Can I take it along to him and see what he says?'

I hesitated, not really wanting to hand it over.

'Can it be mended?' I said doubtfully.

'I don't know for sure. We'll just have to keep our fingers crossed, eh? So I can take your book, all right? I'll make sure you get it back long before it's time for you to go home.'

'My mum's going to be furious,' I said in a very small voice.

'Cheer up, lovie, it's not the end of the world,' she said worriedly.

She felt in her pocket and found a bar of Kit Kat.

'For my coffee break. But you can have it if

you want,' she said, and she pressed it into my hand.

I ate it up quickly before she changed her mind.

Chapter Nine

'Honestly, Stella, you're a hopeless case,' said Miss Hamer-Cotton, waving my activity sheet in front of my nose. 'You can't do Art Art Art, nothing but Art.'

'I like Art,' I said.

'I daresay. But there are heaps of other activities you'll enjoy.'

'I only really like Art,' I said.

Miss Hamer-Cotton looked at me.

'I think you're being a bit awkward, chum,' she said, and she filled in my activity sheet for me.

I found myself being very active indeed. I kept trying to get out of everything but it was no use. I even had to do judo with that awful Jimbo. Louise and Karen thought he was really good looking, especially in his loose white judo clothes, but I couldn't stick him. He was such a show off, bouncing about impressing everyone. Well, he didn't impress me. I stood at the back and deliberately looked the other way when he was demonstrating all the holds.

'Stella! I'd watch carefully if I were you. I'm thinking of pairing you with young James here. He'll flatten you in a flash.'

'You bet! She's wet,' said James, flexing his muscles and grinning. The huge moon of his stomach shone through his judo jacket.

I decided to pay attention. For a couple of minutes. Jimbo was going on about the history of judo and he was being so incredibly boring that I started mimicking him. I copied all his silly gestures and the way he tossed his long fair hair out of his face. The others cottoned on to what I was doing and started giggling. Jimbo started to get seriously annoyed.

He paired us all up to do exercises and I thought for one moment he really might put me with James, but I ended up with Janie instead. Jimbo talked us through all the actions and I pretended not to know my left from my right and my backwards from my forwards so that Janie and I kept collapsing into a giggling heap.

Jimbo didn't find it very funny though. He called me over at the end of the class. I started to get scared but I sauntered over to him as if I couldn't care less.

'Did you enjoy your judo, Stella?' he asked.

I shrugged.

'Did you get anything out of the session?'

'Not really,' I mumbled. 'Only I didn't want to do judo in the first place.'

'Right. Only all the other children *chose* to do judo. Do you think they learned anything today? Or did they just mess about because you were determined to disrupt the whole proceedings?'

'It wasn't just me,' I argued.

Jimbo sighed.

'I don't think I'm going to get anywhere with you, Stella. You'd better go and get changed. What are you doing next?'

'Macramé,' I said, pulling a face.

'You go and tie yourself in a great big knot then,' said Jimbo, ruffling my stubbly hair.

I wondered if he might be quite nice after all. Perhaps I'd try harder in judo. But I couldn't bear to be good in macramé. Jilly was in charge of macramé, and Jilly was *silly*. She wore a flowery smock and sandals and a lot of old grey string jewellery dangled down her big chest. Janie and Rosemary and some of the other little girls wanted to make string necklaces so Jilly got them started off.

Marzipan wanted to make a weird string tassel thing to suspend potted plants in mid air.

'What do you want to make that for?' I whispered. 'It'll look so daft.'

'No it won't. It's for my mum. She likes that sort of thing,' said Marzipan, looking hurt.

'Would you like to try to make one too, Stella?' asked Jilly.

'No thank you.'

'Well, do you want to make a necklace like the others?'

'Not really.'

Jilly folded her arms. 'You've got to make something, Stella. How about a string purse? It could be a present for your mother.'

I didn't feel like making a present for Mum. It was all her fault I was stuck at this horrible summer camp. She'd said I'd enjoy it but I'd decided to hate every minute of it. Some of the others were feeling pretty fed up too. Evergreen wasn't a patch on most summer camps. It was supposed to offer horse riding, but there was just one Shetland pony. There was only one computer too, and it was the cheapest sort so you could only play the most basic games. The swimmers were allowed to canoe in the stream, but it wasn't really deep enough—and the swimming pool wasn't much more than a pond. But it still seemed like Loch Ness to me. I had a swimming session every single day! It was so unfair. I had more swimming sessions than anyone else in the whole camp. Miss Hamer-Cotton said it would help me learn to swim quickly and stop me being frightened of the water. I was sure she was just being horrible and punishing me. So I tried to get my own back by messing about at the pool and not doing what Uncle Ron said. He tried to be all matey at first but eventually he got so cross he made me lose a team point. And then another. Louise and Karen were livid.

I didn't even behave properly in Art. I wasn't just being deliberately naughty. Art at Evergreen was deadly. There wasn't a proper Art room so we were invited to sit in Miss Hamer-Cotton's private sitting room, as if it was some sort of treat. It was a squash on her slippery sofa and our drawing boards kept nudging together. Tinkypoo prowled the carpet, cross because he couldn't curl up on the cushions as usual.

Miss Hamer-Cotton set up a still life on her glass table and said we could sketch it. I didn't want to draw a boring old vase of flowers and an apple and a seashell. None of us did. We started whispering and doing little scribbles and playing noughts and crosses and Miss Hamer-Cotton got cross and said it was a waste of paper.

The next Art session she said we weren't old enough to do a proper still life and she handed round sheets of paper stencilled with drawings from a colouring book. She had wax crayons for the little ones and tiny packs of felt tips for us. There weren't any paints at all. I suppose she didn't want us making a mess on her carpet.

I stared at the felt tips she'd given me. Red, yellow, blue, green, brown, and black. That was all. I thought of my lovely new set of felt tips, all colours of the rainbow.

'Where are you going, Stella?' said Miss Hamer-Cotton.

'I'm just nipping upstairs to my dormi. I want to get my own felt tips,' I said.

'Oh yes, can I get mine too?' asked Louise.

'Can I borrow yours, Louise?' said Karen.

'It's not fair, I didn't bring mine with me,' Janie moaned.

'I'm not allowed to share mine, they're Swiss and very expensive and you have to be careful of the tips,' said Louise.

'That's not fair then, all their pictures will be better than mine,' said Karen. 'It's not fair, is it, Miss Hamer-Cotton?'

'You're right, it's not fair,' said Miss Hamer-Cotton firmly. 'Sit down, Stella. You'll use the felt tip pens I've provided. You'll all use them.'

'But there aren't enough colours,' I moaned.

'You'll just have to be a bit imaginative,' said Miss Hamer-Cotton.

I decided to take her at her word. I'd been given a drawing of a Red Indian, a country landscape, and a comical pig. I coloured the Red Indian in red, giving him scarlet skin, scarlet hair, even scarlet teeth. He was the Reddest Indian ever. I coloured the country landscape red too, pretending that there was an enormous forest fire. I drew little pin-men and pin-cows and pin-sheep and pin-ponies running in all directions shouting help help and moo moo and baa baa and neigh neigh. I coloured the comical pig very carefully indeed with little red dots so that he came out a pretty pink, and then I drew clothes on top. I dressed my pig in a baggy tracksuit with H.C. stitched on the pocket and I drew a cross little cat perching on the pig's shoulders.

Miss Hamer-Cotton noticed everyone giggling at my colouring and came to have a look. I tried

to crumple up the pig quickly but she took it away from me and straightened it out and saw for herself why they were giggling.

'I've just about had enough of you, Stella Stebbings,' she said wearily. 'I don't think it's very funny. I don't think the Emeralds are going to find it very funny either when I take away yet another team point.'

'That's not fair,' said Louise furiously. 'Why should we keep losing team points just because Stella's so stupid? Why can't you just punish her? Make her do extra swimming or something, she hates that.'

'Perhaps that's a good idea, Louise,' said Miss Hamer-Cotton.

'But I do extra swimming already! You can't make me do any more!' I said, horrified.

'Oh yes I can,' said Miss Hamer-Cotton. 'You can miss Art altogether and do two swimming sessions a day until you can learn to behave yourself.'

Louise and Karen were grinning all over their faces. I couldn't bear it.

'I won't! You can't make me! You're not even in charge. I want to see the Brigadier,' I shouted.

'All right then,' said Miss Hamer-Cotton. 'You come with me. You shall see the Brigadier.'

Chapter Ten

I was really scared. I'd only seen glimpses of the Brigadier so far, but that was enough. He was very tall and his hair was very short and he looked as if he could be very strict indeed. He'd shouted at some boys because they ran through a flower bed and he certainly sounded strict too.

'I didn't really mean it,' I said, when we were out in the corridor.

But Miss Hamer-Cotton was still pink as a prawn with temper.

'*I* meant it,' she said. 'Come on.'

She took hold of me and ushered me along the corridor.

'I don't want to be a nuisance and bother the Brigadier,' I said.

'You can't seem to help being a nuisance, Stella. But perhaps father will be able to knock some sense into you.'

Knock some sense! Goodness, what was he going to do to me? I pictured the Brigadier in boxing gloves, pummelling me. No, he wouldn't really hit me. It wouldn't be allowed. But how could I stop him if he tried?

I wanted Mum. I even wanted Uncle Bill. I was in such a state that when Miss Hamer-Cotton marched me down the forbidden right-hand corridor towards the tower I began to think she might really lock me up.

'I'm sorry,' I said. 'I'm really sorry.'

'So you should be,' said Miss Hamer-Cotton grimly.

'Can we go back now?'

'No. You asked to see the Brigadier and see him you shall.'

Miss Hamer-Cotton opened a heavy wooden door marked Private at the end of the corridor. She pulled me through it and up a narrow flight of winding stairs. We were in the tower.

I wondered about trying to make a run for it. Princess Stellarina would have done. But I didn't really know where to run to. I was trapped in the tower with Hag Hateful-Catty and any minute now I was going to be in the power of the dreaded Brigavampire himself.

Miss Hamer-Cotton paused at the top of the stairs and knocked at another big wooden door. She waited. I held my breath. She knocked again.

'Are you there, father?'

I shut my eyes and made the biggest wish in

the world that he wasn't. But it was no use. I heard a terrifying rumble from behind the door.

Miss Hamer-Cotton opened it.

'Stella Stebbings would like a word with you,' she said, and she pushed me into the room.

It was a weird round dark room, rather like an old junk shop, crammed with all sorts of books and bits. There were lots of things I'd have liked to look at properly but I was too frightened of the Brigadier to do anything but stand and stare at him. He stared back at me. He was sitting behind a big old desk, drumming his fingers on a leather blotting pad.

'Well?' he said.

I trod on the rubbery ends of my trainers and said nothing.

'I believe you want to say something?' he said.

'Not really,' I whispered.

'Then why did you come to see me?'

'Miss Hamer-Cotton sort of made me,' I mumbled.

'Aha. I gather you're in some sort of trouble?'

'Well. Mmm. Actually, yes.'

'Would you care to elucidate?'

I wasn't very sure what that meant, but I knew I didn't really want to do it anyway, so I shook my head.

'Which team are you in, Miss Stebbings?'

No one had ever called me Miss Stebbings before. It sounded most peculiar.

'Emerald.'

'Oh dear. I believe the Emeralds are flagging rather badly at the moment. They're bottom, aren't they?'

'Mmm.'

'Well, if you keep getting into trouble then you'll lose a team point and the Emeralds will flag even more.'

I shifted about uncomfortably. His eyes narrowed.

'Have you lost a team point already, Miss Stebbings?'

I nodded.

'More than one?'

I nodded again.

'A recalcitrant offender,' said the Brigadier.

I didn't know what that meant either.

'So what are we going to do with you, hmm?'

There was a long pause.

'Don't you like it here?' he said.

'No.' I said it before I could stop myself.

The Brigadier looked a bit taken aback.

'No? Yet you wanted to come here, didn't you?'

'No. Mum made me. Because she's having a honeymoon with Uncle Bill.'

'Oh. I see.'

There was another pause. The Brigadier didn't

look as if he knew what to say next. He started fiddling with the bits on his desk. There were some toy soldiers and a jar of pens and a brass paper knife and some old *National Geographic* magazines and lots of letters and a big photograph in a silver frame. It was of a very pretty lady. It certainly wasn't Miss Hamer-Cotton.

'Can't you make the best of things now you're here, Miss Stebbings?'

'Mmm. Only . . . only it's not fair.'

'What isn't?'

'Swimming.' Now I was started I couldn't stop. 'She makes me go swimming every single day even though I hate it, and none of the others have to do it that much, she's just picking on me and now she says I've got to do two rotten swimming sessions each day and it's no *use*, I can't swim, and I won't ever be able to swim and Mum promised I wouldn't have to, she wrote you a letter and—'

He lifted one long finger in the air and I managed to stop. I couldn't quite believe I'd said it all. The little room still seemed full of the sound of my voice.

'A letter, you say?'

'Mmm, from my mother. And Mum had a word with her too, and she said—'

The finger went up again.

'I take it you are referring to Miss Hamer-Cotton when you keep using the female pronoun?'

I guessed the female pronoun meant 'she'. I knew grown-ups thought it rude to say 'she' although I'd never worked out why. I nodded and was about to start again but his finger went to his lips.

'Let me find this letter first.' He searched his desk and eventually found it beneath his blotter. I edged away while he was looking for it. I peered at the books on the shelves nearest me. They looked very boring, all about War and History and Geography.

'Here we are. One letter. And yes, your mother does mention the fact that you are worried about swimming. Hmm.' He moved a toy soldier around on his desk, almost as if he was taking him for a little walk.

'So please, Mr Brigadier, do I have to go on having swimming lessons?' I asked. I wanted to sound extra polite to try to get round him, but I knew by the expression on his face that I'd said something else wrong.

'Don't you want to learn to swim?'

I shook my head vigorously.

'Supposing you fall in a river or a pond or whatever? Wouldn't swimming prove to be a useful accomplishment?'

'I'd sooner steer clear of all rivers and ponds.'

I wasn't trying to be funny but he actually

104

laughed. I cheered up because I thought he might be on my side now, but then he spoilt it all.

'I think it would be a good idea if you kept up the swimming sessions all the same. One a day. Perhaps two might prove a bit too much—for Uncle Ron, if not for you.'

'It's not fair,' I mumbled.

'Life isn't fair, Miss Stebbings,' he said in that infuriating grown-up way.

But then he looked at his photograph.

'Life isn't fair,' he repeated sadly.

I wondered if the lady was his wife. I guessed she was dead now. I went all hot and embarrassed, terrified that he might start talking about her or crying or something. I leaned against the books, trying to think of something to say.

'Hey, watch those spines!' he said in a very different sort of voice.

'Oh. Sorry.' I stopped lounging.

'One should always treat books with respect,' he said, still stern.

'I know,' I said. 'I've got a book like that. An antiquarian book. It's called *Fifty Favourite Fairy Tales*, my mother bought it for me and it's got masses of colour plates and—' And I remembered what had happened to it.

'And?' said the Brigadier.

I looked down at my feet.

105

'Nothing,' I mumbled.

'Fairy stories, eh?'

'Mmm,' I said, wishing I'd kept my mouth shut. What was I going to do if he asked to see it?

'Were there any Fairy Godfathers in this fairy story book of yours?' he asked.

I stared at him.

'Not that I can think of. Fairy Godmothers. But you don't get godfathers, not fairy ones.'

'Don't you?' said the Brigadier. He opened a drawer of his desk and took out a book. An old blue leather book. I looked at the gold lettering. *Fifty Favourite Fairy Tales*. My book! But it wasn't ripped to pieces. The binding was perfect. It was as good as new.

The Brigadier held it out to me, smiling. I took the book, my hands trembling.

'Is it mine? But it can't be. It's not torn any more. How did it happen?'

'Magic?'

I wasn't that daft. I looked very carefully at the spine. The leather was the same colour as the front and the back but it was softer and more supple and when I peered right up close I could see tiny join lines where someone had patiently matched the torn old leather with the new.

'You mended it for me,' I said.

'Mrs Markham brought it straight to me.' (Orange

106

Overall/Purple Pinafore/Dotty Dress). 'She told me the awful facts of the case and I decided to help as best I could.'

'These awful facts,' I said worriedly. 'Does she know who spoilt my book?'

The Brigadier made an arch of his fingers and rested his chin on it.

'I wouldn't enquire further, if I were you. Just be thankful that the book is very nearly back to rights.'

'Oh I am thankful. I'm ever so thankful,' I said, beaming at him.

'So how about doing something for me in return?' said the Brigadier.

I looked at him.

'Those swimming lessons,' I said dolefully.

'That's my girl.'

I sighed.

'Cheer up. It's not as bad as all that. And there are all the other activities too.'

I wrinkled my nose. I didn't mean him to see, but his eyes were too sharp.

'Don't you think much of them either?'

'I don't like judo. Or macramé.'

'What *do* you like?'

There was another pause.

'I like making up stories,' I eventually decided.

'Do you?' He stared at his desk thoughtfully.

He stared at the *National Geographic* magazines. 'What about you starting up your own magazine while you're here? An Evergreen Magazine, with you as the editor. Does the idea appeal?'

It did. Very much indeed.

Chapter Eleven

I sat cross-legged on my bed in the Emerald dormi, doodling with my new felt tips on a pad of rough paper. It was Marzipan's pad actually, but I was sure she wouldn't mind. I wrote my name in bright pink and outlined it in magenta. It looked very stylish. I tried a wavy emerald green line round the magenta and then edged that with midnight blue. The STELLA was a little blurred now but it still looked impressive.

I wondered about calling my magazine *Stella*. I thought about it, colouring until the midnight blue seeped right through the page and blotched the one underneath. I wanted my magazine to be grander than a comic. But I wanted to show it was *mine*.

I thought some more, doodling. I doodled faces and flowers, smiley suns and stars. Stars. I'd looked up Stella once in a book of girls' names. It was a Latin word and it meant star.

'Star,' I whispered, smiling.

I turned to a fresh piece of paper and printed the word in giant crimson capitals. I filled them in with little silver sparkly stars. Well, they were grey pencil really because I didn't have a special silver crayon. Then I got my felt tips and drew a whole galaxy of multi-coloured stars filling up the whole page. I sang star songs as I coloured. *Twinkle twinkle little star. Star of Wonder, star of might. Star light, star bright, first little star I see tonight.* Inside the darkness of my head ideas sparkled like the Milky Way.

I was having such a lovely time I was annoyed when the others came trooping into the dormi.

'There she is! Did you get into trouble then, Baldy?' Karen demanded. 'What was the Brigadier like? Did he get really cross?'

'Nope. He was very nice,' I said, grinning at Karen's disappointment.

'Well, you're still in trouble with Miss Hamer-Cotton. She went looking for you when you didn't come back to Art,' said Karen triumphantly. 'She's furious with you, isn't she, Louise?'

'I think we ought to boot Baldy out of the Emerald team altogether,' said Louise, jogging me on purpose as she went past.

'See if I care,' I said serenely, doing a golden rain of stars with my yellow ochre.

'Didn't you really get into trouble?' Marzipan whispered. 'Hey, Stella, is that my pad?'

'You don't mind, do you?'

'Well, you've used up rather a lot of paper,' said Marzipan reproachfully.

'Yes, what's she been drawing?' said Karen, snatching. 'What's all this star rubbish?'

'It's a design, Karen,' I said. 'For a magazine cover.'

'What magazine?'

'*My* magazine,' I said. 'I'm starting a magazine. A proper one for the whole of Evergreen.'

'Who says?'

'The Brigadier, that's who,' I said.

'Why don't you pull the other one, it's got bells on,' said Karen pathetically.

'You go and ask the Brigadier then. You'll see,' I said, colouring away.

'But why are you doing this magazine? You're the one who keeps messing about and getting into trouble. You've lost heaps of team points. Why should you get to do a magazine?' Karen demanded furiously. 'It's not fair.'

I remembered what the Brigadier had said to me.

'Life isn't fair, Karen,' I chortled.

'You think you're so clever,' said Karen. 'You make me sick. Your magazine's going to be a right mess. Isn't it, Louise?'

'Is my rough pad going to be your magazine?' asked Marzipan.

'Well—I expect I'll get some proper paper later on, but can I go on borrowing your pad meanwhile?'

'I suppose so,' said Marzipan, sighing.

'I'll let you do a special bit in my magazine. What do you fancy doing? A poem? A story?'

'I can't make them up like you,' said Marzipan, lying on her bed and reaching for her book. 'I don't like writing stories, I just like reading them. Here, is your magazine going to have Book Reviews? I could write about *Little Women*, it's my favourite book.'

'OK,' I said. I thought Book Reviews sounded a bit dull, but it was her rough pad after all.

'Are you going to have a Fashion Page?' asked Janie. 'Oh go on, please, Stella. I could do all drawings of new fashions, I'm quite good at that. Can I?'

'All right. But you'll have to do them really carefully.'

'Here, Baldy, are you going to have Hairdressing Hints?' Karen called. 'I can just see it. Baldy's Beauty Column. You too can have hair as long and luxuriant as mine if you use Sulphuric Acid Shampoo, says Boring Baldy Show-off Stebbings.'

I waggled my tongue at her, too busy to be bothered to fight. I scribbled down our names in a column.

'Right. I'm the editor. Marzipan can be in charge of the Book Page. Janie can do some Fashion.'

'Can I do something, Stella?' Rosemary begged. 'I can't do joined up writing yet, but it doesn't matter, does it? Can I write about Dora? I could write about how you rescued her, Stella. I'd do it ever so carefully and you could tell me how to spell all the long words. Please let me, Stella, I know I could tell it all.'

'You've told it all. Repeatedly,' said Karen. 'Who wants to hear that old story again? Honestly, you're all mad. Why do you want to write for her daft old magazine? It'll just be rubbish. Won't it be rubbish, Louise?'

'What about the boys?' said Janie. 'Are you going to get them to write for the magazine too? That James could do you a poem, couldn't he?'

'Do we have to have the boys? They'll just mess about,' said Marzipan.

'I'll see,' I said grandly. 'There's not going to be much left for them to do. I'm going to do a story and then there's the Stars page, I want to do that too, and then if we have Book Reviews we might as well have Film Reviews, and I could do that, easy-peasy. What else do you have in a magazine? I suppose we could get Alan to do a sports page.'

'I'll do the sports page,' said Louise.

I stared at her.

'I know more about sports than anyone else, don't I?' said Louise, idly picking up her tennis racket and bouncing a ball up and down on the strings.

She was right. And it was a major triumph, Louise actually wanting to write for my magazine.

'OK, Louise. You're the sports correspondent,' I agreed.

Karen had gone very red. She looked as if she might be trying hard not to cry.

'You can be on the magazine too, Karen,' said Marzipan.

'Here, I'm the editor,' I said.

'Don't worry, I wouldn't write for your daft old magazine even if you went down on your knees and begged,' Karen shouted, and she ran out of the room.

We soon forgot about her because we were so busy. I had great fun writing the Stars page, especially the horoscope for my own birthsign, Sagittarius.

'You are at the start of a brilliant career. At last everyone will recognize your true talents. Do not be deterred by hostility. They are only jealous. You have a really starry future. Warning: avoid water at all costs!'

Then I settled down to do my Star Film Review. I drew a big screen taking up nearly all the page on Marzipan's pad and then did a border of all the delicious food you get to eat in the cinema, popcorn and Mars bars and Magnum icecreams and hot dogs and Coke and ice lollies. Then I started writing my review inside the screen—and that was when I got stuck.

My all-time favourite film was *Curse of the Killer Vampire Bats*. Mum bought it for me by mistake. She found a whole pile of children's videos at £1 a time at a Car Boot Sale and gave them to me to keep me quiet. They were mostly babyish cartoons and I fidgeted and fussed throughout—but when

115

I watched *Curse of the Killer Vampire Bats* I stayed still as a mouse and didn't so much as squeak. It was certainly *not* a children's video. It had got put in this Kute Kartoons for Kiddies case by mistake.

I couldn't believe my luck. It was so wonderfully scary. I *loved* the Killer Vampire Bats. They started off as furry little Vampire Bat Babies with weeny teeny teeth, but then they grew and grew and grew. Their teeth turned into the sharpest fangs ever so they could rip your head off your neck with one bite.

Mum just about died when she saw what I was watching and threw it in the dustbin. I was furious with her—but she couldn't stop me buying my own toy rubber vampire bat with my pocket money. I called him Bloodsucker and decided he was a distant wicked relation of Squeakycheese. I encouraged Bloodsucker in his evil habits for all I was worth. Mum had just started to go out with Uncle Bill then. Bloodsucker decided he simply couldn't stick Uncle Bill. He kept attacking him like crazy, going for his neck.

Mum said if I couldn't control Bloodsucker he was going in the dustbin too. I knew she meant it, so Bloodsucker decided Uncle Bill's blood was too watery for his taste. He had a happy time in my toy cupboard instead, gorging on all my old discarded Barbies.

But now I was stuck writing my review of *Curse of the Killer Vampire Bats* because Mum had thrown it away when I was only halfway through watching it. I needed to know what happened at the end. I asked everyone if they'd ever seen a truly super film called *Curse of the Killer Vampire Bats* but nobody else had seen it. Then Rosemary smiled.

'*I've* seen it, Stella,' she said.

'Are you sure?' I said doubtfully.

'Yes. I remember the vampire bat. I couldn't watch much. I had to go behind the sofa.'

She was taking a break from writing DORA'S DRAMMATIK RESKU because her wrist was aching so she was busy tidying Dora's bed.

'She's got it in such a mess, I just don't know what she's been up to,' said Rosemary primly. 'Naughty Dora.'

'I'm not at all surprised you had to go behind the sofa. *I* was just a little bit frightened of *Curse of the Killer Vampire Bats*,' I admitted.

'Dora was *terribly* frightened,' said Rosemary, making her donkey shake all over. 'They attacked a cow.'

'A cow?' I said. 'You mean . . . a naughty lady?'

'No. A real cow. And Dora and I thought if those vampire bats could attack a cow they might easily go for a donkey.'

'There weren't any cows in *Curse of the Killer*

Vampire Bats,' I said. 'There were lots of ladies in nighties and they all died horribly, blood dribbling down their chests.'

'I didn't see any ladies in nighties,' said Rosemary.

'Yes. Well. You were behind the sofa.'

'But I was listening. There was just this one man. And the vampire bats. On the telly.'

It turned out she'd been watching some little *nature* programme.

'You are an *idiot*, Rosemary,' I said impatiently.

'Don't be mean to me, Stella. You'll upset Dora,' said Rosemary, making the donkey droop.

'Cheer up, Dora,' I said quickly.

'She's too unhappy now. Look, she's sobbing,' said Rosemary, making little sniffy noises and helping Dora wipe her eyes with her front hooves.

I was getting a bit fed up with all this.

'She's *yawning* now,' I said, snatching Dora and making her mouth gape. 'She's terribly tired. I think we'd better pop her into bed now.'

'No! Don't put Dora into bed,' Rosemary squealed, snatching her away.

'Why not?' I asked, startled.

Rosemary shuffled right up to me and whispered in my ear. 'She's wet it.'

I giggled. 'No she hasn't. She's completely house-trained and—'

'She's really wet it, Stella. Look,' Rosemary whispered, holding up the old cardigan.

So I looked. And examined it. Rosemary was right.

'Rosemary!'

Rosemary shrugged helplessly.

'You didn't—?'

'No!'

'Then—?'

We both looked at Dora. Her head still drooped, as if in shame.

'This is ridiculous,' I said.

I wondered if it could have been Tinkypoo. But he never came near our dormi. It was a mystery.

The plot of *Curse of the Killer Vampire Bats* remained a mystery too. In the end I just wrote, '*Curse of the Killer Vampire Bats* is the best film I've ever seen. If you see it you will be scared senseless.' I drew a picture of Bloodsucker grinning wickedly and coloured all round his mouth very red indeed.

It was getting near lunch time but I got started on my story, copying out Princess Stellarina from my red and black notebook.

'You've got your own notebook, you could have done the magazine in that,' said Marzipan reproachfully.

'Yes, but I've written out my Stellarina story in it, I've used up heaps of pages.'

'You're using up heaps of my pages now,' said Marzipan. 'What are you copying out?'

'My Princess Stellarina story. It's going to be the special Star Story now.'

'Oh goody goody,' said Rosemary, tucking Dora into a new bed of clean T-shirt and knickers.

'You can't put that story in your magazine,' said Marzipan. 'The Brigadier and Miss Hamer-Cotton and Uncle Ron might want to have a read of it. They'll have a fit. They'll see you're making fun of them. Oh, Stella, you can't!'

'Yes, I can,' I said—but when I read the whole story through I started to worry. Perhaps I could cross out the Brigavampire parts. The Brigadier was sort of my friend now. I could leave in the bits about Hag Hateful-Catty—although she *was* the Brigadier's daughter. Well, at least I could keep the Uncle Pong parts. Or could I? Uncle Ron kept swearing he'd have me swimming like a little seal by the time I went home. I still couldn't swim more than two strokes at a time and I kept going under and choking—but when I was nearly crying Uncle Ron ducked under the water and came up blowing bubbles so that I laughed instead.

I sighed now and ripped out my Stellarina story from the magazine. I'd have to think of something else instead.

Chapter Twelve

I brooded about my story over lunch and let my meal go cold. It didn't really matter. The fishfingers were lukewarm to start with and so undercooked that I couldn't help imagining the cold slimy little things still had tails and fins and beady eyes underneath the breadcrumbs. I prodded them dubiously and reached for my pudding. It was jam tart, a smear of strawberry on great grey paving-stone pastry and the custard had sickened in its jug and developed hard skin and boils.

I made this joke and everyone groaned and stopped eating except James.

'Honestly, James, how can you eat it?' I said, staring in horrified fascination as he dipped a fish-finger into custard and ate both with relish.

'I'm hungry, see,' said James, his mouth full. 'But I agree, this tuck is horrible muck. It's even worse than my school and that's breaking the rule. That's just zero zero zero stars in my personal Bad Food Guide. This is zero zero zero *zilch*, I must confide.'

I had a sudden idea.

'James, you're interested in food, aren't you?'

'You'd be a twit not to notice it,' said James.

'Can you do any cooking?'

'Mmm,' said James, nodding.

'You cook?' said Richard, sniggering. 'A boy cooking! What a cissy.'

'Of course I can, it's a job for a man,' said James. 'A chef is a bloke and that's not a joke.'

'You wouldn't like to write a cookery page for my magazine, would you?' I asked eagerly.

'I'll write you a page for a very large wage.'

'I can't pay you anything!'

'Then I won't do it and you just blew it.'

'Oh do stop those silly rhymes, they don't half get on my nerves. Look, I'm not paying any of the others anything so why should I pay you? Please do it, James. Go on. It'd be ever so good.'

I tried flattering him like anything but I couldn't get round him. I asked Marzipan and some of the other girls if they could do it instead, but none of us knew much about cooking.

Then the next morning I got a present from Mum and Uncle Bill. They were spending the first few days of their honeymoon in Paris and so they sent me a real French can-can dancer doll. She had feathers in her hair and a frilly pink skirt like a lampshade. I lifted up the pink ruffles to see what sort of knickers she was wearing and discovered that she didn't even have legs, let alone knickers. The space underneath her skirt was filled with a cone of chocolates wrapped in pink foil paper.

I tried one straight away but it was a bit of a disappointment. It was plain chocolate for a start and the filling was flavoured with liqueur or something that made it taste bitter. I let Marzipan have a nibble and she didn't like it much either.

But I knew who might like it. I did a little bargaining with James and he eventually agreed to write a cookery page for a fee of five French chocolates.

'Though it's not much of a wage. And what sort of cookery page?' said James, munching.

'I don't know. It's up to you. Do me a recipe for something. Only don't do it in rhyme, that's all I ask.'

James went away and wrote me out a recipe for Special Star biscuits. I thought that was a smashing idea but when I read it through I couldn't understand half of it because it was full of those weird cookery words that always get me muddled. How can you *cream* butter and sugar? And how do you leave to cool? Does that mean put in fridge? How cool is cool?

James sighed and said I was as thick as a brick

but when I gave him two more chocolates he wrote it all out again using ordinary words I could understand.

STAR BISCUITS.
A RECIPE FOR COMPLETE IDIOTS

Things you need to make the biscuits:
4 oz butter (just cut one packet in half)
4 oz caster sugar (if you haven't got scales to
    weigh it on then it's four heaped table-
    spoons. They're the great big ones you
    can't get right into your mouth)
8 oz plain flour (measure in same way)
5 oz icing sugar (measure ditto)
1 egg
1 tube of little silver balls for decoration
1 Jiffy lemon

Right. First switch on the oven at 375 F.
This can heat up nicely while you make the biscuits. Don't take all day or you'll be wasting electricity. You take the butter and the caster sugar first. (Not the icing sugar. Guess what. That is for icing the biscuits.) You shove the butter and caster sugar in a big bowl and beat them around

with a wooden spoon. They stick together in lumps and it looks as if it isn't going to work but carry on mixing them and quite soon they blend together and go all soft and creamy and smooth. Then you add the flour and mix that around too until it all looks the same colour. Then in another bowl crack the egg (just bash it on the side of the bowl and let it slurp out *inside* the bowl, not outside) and beat it up with a fork until it stops looking disgusting and is a nice frothy yellow. Then add the egg into the bowl of butter, sugar, and flour. It goes all oozy and you have to beat it around quite a bit with the spoon. You can also do it with your hand but if so make sure your hands are clean. No one wants little bits of fluff or grit or worse lurking in their biscuit. When it is all smooth like soft plasticine you get a rolling pin. Roll the nice squidgy mixture on a clean surface on which you've sprinkled a little bit of flour. You can sprinkle flour on your rolling pin too. Only a bit, don't make it look as if it's snowing. Then roll it out carefully. You *must* know how to roll, if not you're too thick to make biscuits, you probably don't even know how to *eat* them. When it's all smooth and as flat as you can get it without it developing holes then use a cutter. Ideally you need a cutter in the shape of a star. If you haven't got one maybe you could use a round jampot lid and then snip into the circle with scissors turning it into a star. This might make the stars a bit lopsided but have a go. Then you smear a bit of old butter or marge all over a baking tray (great if you can just use the wrapper round the butter). This is to make the tray slippery so the biscuits won't stick when they're cooked. Put the star shapes on the greased baking tray. Leave a biscuit-sized gap between each one because they spread out a lot as they cook. Then put them in the oven on one of the little shelves. Not right at the top or they might burn. Make sure you close the door properly. They take about 8–10 minutes to cook. While they are doing this then you're supposed to wash up. I don't always. About 8 minutes after you've put the biscuits in they start to smell delicious. You can open the oven door and peep at them to make sure they're not going too brown. If they're still very pale then they obviously aren't cooked yet. Wait another couple of minutes and try again. *Careful* when you take them out the oven.

You'll need an oven glove or an old towel. You can't touch a red hot baking tray with your bare hands. Well, you can, but you have to go around in bandages for weeks. So, you take the baking tray out. The biscuits will still be softish so don't poke them about too much. Leave them for five or ten minutes so they can harden up a bit. Slide a fish slice or a flat knife under them gently one by one and put them on a wire mesh cooking thing. If you haven't got one then use the wire tray inside the grill pan. Anyway, leave the biscuits to cool a bit more, at least ten minutes. While they are cooling it's time to mix the icing sugar. This is the best bit. You have to put the 5 oz through a sieve into a bowl. It doesn't flop through all at once. You have to encourage it by rubbing it through with a spoon. When it's all in the bowl you add about one tablespoonful of Jiffy lemon juice. You can add plain water instead, but lemon gives a much better taste. Don't add it all at once. Icing sugar is horribly deceptive. You can add one little squeeze and it seems to disappear into the sugar but when you mix it around with a spoon it suddenly goes all sloppy and runny

127

and useless. So not more than a tablespoon of lemon juice and mix it around and around with a metal spoon until *eventually* it's smooth. You shouldn't be able to pour it like milk, sort of ooze it like cream. I'd spread it on the biscuits with a knife, it's less messy. Do not have too many sly licks or there won't be enough. Then dot your little silver balls over the icing. Then EAT them.

When I'd read it all through I gave James another chocolate for luck.

'Here, why's old Fatso getting all your chocolates, Stella?' said Alan. 'I'll do something for your magazine if you like.'

He did a carefully drawn comic strip. I knew he'd copied part of it from the *Beano* but I gave him a chocolate anyway. Then I had to give one to Bilbo too because he'd got Alan to help him print some silly old jokes we'd all heard hundreds of times already. Bilbo didn't even like his chocolate and was rude enough to spit it straight out.

Richard helped Louise with her sports column and he also did his own Sports Star quiz. I didn't know any of the answers and I didn't think many of the others would either but I quite liked the idea of a quiz. I decided to make it a great big All

Stars Quiz and I got everyone to help me make up questions on Television Stars and Film Stars and Pop Stars. Nearly everyone. Karen was still sulking and wouldn't join in.

I certainly didn't care. My magazine was coming along splendidly. I even thought of a new Star Story. The idea came to me when I was looking at my beautifully repaired book at bedtime. I'd always liked the baddies in the fairy tales much more than all those whimpering princesses and simpering princes. So I decided to write my own Topsy-Turvy tales for the magazine. I had Fifty Favourite Topsy-Turvy Tales as my first title. A few days later I changed it to Fifteen Favourite Topsy-Turvy tales.

It actually ended up as Five Favourite Topsy-Turvy tales. I wrote about the wolf gobbling up the grandmother and Little Red Riding Hood *and* the woodcutter, Rumpelstiltskin leaving that silly girl to do her own spinning and skipping off with all the gold, the Three Bears catching Goldilocks and pelting her with porridge, the Ugly Sisters one at a time cramming their great fat feet into the glass slipper and sharing the handsome prince between them, and the giant squashing Jack into squidge with one great stamp of his boot.

Chapter Thirteen

When I'd used up nearly all the pages of Marzipan's rough pad I went and showed my *Star* magazine to the Brigadier. I hoped he'd read it from cover to cover but I suppose he didn't really have the time. But he did spend quite a while flicking through and sometimes he stopped and read a whole page. I was pleased to see that they were nearly always the pages I had written. Sometimes he smiled and once he laughed out loud.

'Do you think it's OK?' I asked.

He smiled. 'I think it's more than OK, Miss Stebbings. I think it's a magazine to be proud of. You have a word with my daughter, see if she can get busy with the photocopier.'

'What, so that I can sell it like a real magazine?' I said eagerly.

'I don't see why not,' said the Brigadier. 'How's the swimming going?' he added, as I was halfway out of his door.

I pulled a face.

'It's not.'

'But you're still trying?'

'Every day. But it doesn't work. I know what to do with my arms and legs and I blow when I'm supposed to but I still go glug glug glug.'

'Don't worry, you'll get the hang of it eventually,' said the Brigadier.

I knew I wouldn't—but I also knew it was a waste of breath arguing. I ran off to ask Miss Hamer-Cotton to get printing my lovely Star magazine straight away.

I hoped she'd do it there and then but it took her four whole *days*—and then I couldn't help being bitterly disappointed. I know it was daft, but I'd expected her to make some proper magazines with coloured covers and real pages. These limp little stapled sheets of messy handwriting looked like something from school. But all the other children started sharing them out, wanting to have a look, and they seemed really interested, so I cheered up.

'Hey, give those back. They're not free handouts, you know. They're for sale. One pound per copy. All right, all right, fifty pence. But you're getting an absolute bargain.'

I sold every single copy in a morning and went back to Miss Hamer-Cotton for some more.

She sighed.

'Oh, Stella. It took me ages to do the last lot—especially all that stapling. Can't you all share the copies I've already done?'

'Well, not really, Miss Hamer-Cotton. They're for sale, you see, and it wouldn't be fair on the children who've already bought their own copies.' I hesitated as she looked dazed. 'You wouldn't like to buy a copy for yourself, would you?'

I wasn't sure whether she was going to laugh or get cross.

'You really are the limit,' she said. 'And you shouldn't have sold the copies, Stella. What have you done with the money?'

I patted my bulging pockets. I sounded just like 'Jingle Bells'.

'I'm not sure you ought to keep the money for yourself,' said Miss Hamer-Cotton.

'Well, I was planning to pay my staff a sort of wage.'

'What about your printer?' said Miss Hamer-Cotton.

'Oh. Well. How much would you like?'

'I was only joking, Stella. At least I think I was. But I really think you ought to make a large donation to a children's charity.'

'Charity begins at home,' I mumbled, but I didn't dare say it out loud.

I ended up putting a few pounds in the charity

box, but Miss Hamer-Cotton let me keep the rest.

On Saturday morning we were allowed to walk into the village with Jimbo and Jilly. I went to the newsagent and bought Marzipan a new jotter (it was quite a bit smaller but she said she didn't mind) and some fruit gums and chocolate drops and chocolate toffees and jelly babies and big wiggly jelly snakes—a huge bag of all the sweets that I love and Mum won't let me buy because she says they'll rot my teeth. I'd much sooner have false teeth and eat fruit gums and chocolate drops and chocolate toffees and jelly babies and big wiggly jelly snakes every day. Marzipan bought a big Yorkie bar and Janie and Rosemary bought crisps and a big bottle of lemonade.

Louise and Karen hadn't bothered to come to the shops with us.

'Won't they be jealous when we have an absolute feast,' I said.

But when we got back to the Emerald dormi we found Louise and Karen having their own private feast. Louise's dad had sent her a huge box of crystallized fruit. Karen was back in favour and was slobbering at a great pink pear, sugar crystals all round her mouth.

'See what *we've* got, Baldy,' she said.

'I don't care. I don't like that stuff anyway,' I said.

I did really. Uncle Bill had bought some crystallized apricots round last Christmas and they were the most beautiful sweets I'd ever eaten, like little sugar suns. Louise was eating an apricot now and it made my mouth water just watching.

I looked at my sweets. I looked at the chocolate and the crisps. I looked and looked at the crystallized fruit.

'You know what we should do,' I said. 'Have a midnight feast.'

Karen looked at Louise. Louise was no fool.

'I think a midnight feast is a rather babyish idea, if you ask me,' she said. 'We won't bother, will we, Karen?'

'No, that's right, we won't bother,' said Karen. 'Who wants to go to a silly old midnight feast, eh?'

'Marzipan and Janie and Rosemary and I do, don't we?' I said.

'Wow, that would be great, Stella. Yummy yummy,' said Janie.

'Dora can come too, can't she?' said Rosemary. She hesitated. 'What is a midnight feast?'

'We get up at midnight and have a feast, of course,' I said.

'Are you just playing, Stella?' Marzipan asked, looking worried.

'No, I mean it. We're having a midnight feast. Tonight!'

'We'll get into awful trouble if we get found out,' said Marzipan.

'We're not going to get found out.'

'What if we all get the giggles and Miss Hamer-Cotton hears?'

'She won't. Oh don't spoil it, Marzie. It's going to be such fun.'

It didn't feel like fun when my alarm clock went off at midnight. I'd only just got to sleep for a start. The girls in boarding school books who have midnight feasts always hide their alarm clocks under their pillows. Well I tried but it was so uncomfortable I couldn't stand it. I have this great big Popeye alarm clock which digs in horribly. It's got such a loud ring that I didn't dare put it up on my chest of drawers as usual in case it woke Miss Hamer-Cotton too. I tried setting it and cramming it inside a drawer but the ring was so muffled beneath all my jumpers and jeans that I was scared I'd sleep right through it.

So in the end I had to turf poor old Squeakycheese out of my bed and curl up with the alarm clock clasped to my chest. It was very cold and very hard. So as I said, I didn't get to sleep for ages and then Popeye's muscley arms ticked round to twelve o'clock and he rang the bell for all he was worth. It vibrated right through me and I lay twitching with shock. I felt so terrible I thought I might be ill. My eyes were all hot and burny, my head ached and I felt sick. I wanted to turn over and go back to sleep more than anything else in the whole world. But I was determined to have a midnight feast even if it killed me.

I sat up and scratched my tufts.

'Wakey wakey,' I whispered into the dark dormi. 'It's midnight. Time for our feast.'

Someone muttered. Someone mumbled. But no one moved.

'Come on,' I said, and I stuck my legs out of bed. 'Midnight. Listen to the clock. Dong, dong, dong, dong, dong—'

'Stella!'

'Dong, etc.,' I said. 'Next up after me gets first pick at my sweets, OK?'

'Me!' Rosemary shouted, jumping out of bed.

'Sh! Keep your voices down, *please*,' Marzipan hissed, getting up too.

Rosemary chose a handful of chocolate drops. She gave a pretend nibble to Dora and a real nibble to Janie. Karen sat up in bed, peering through the gloom. She watched us for a couple of minutes without saying anything and then she leant over towards Louise's bed.

'Are you awake?' she whispered hopefully.

'Mmm. We might as well join in too,' said Louise. 'We'll never get any sleep with this row going on.'

She was too mean to donate any of her crystallized fruit to the feast, but she did get out the tin containing her iced cake. There wasn't much of it left now but I suppose it was better than nothing. I'd slipped a large slab of the teatime cake up my T-shirt so I got that out too, and all my sweets and Marzipan's chocolate and the crisps and lemonade. It was really quite a respectable feast.

'And look what else I've got,' I said, and I produced a very sticky pot of strawberry jam.

I'd taken that at teatime too and it had made a right mess of my T-shirt.

'Stella, you are dreadful!' said Marzipan.

'I'll put it back again tomorrow. I just thought

138

a bit of jam might make this dry old cake a bit tastier, that's all.'

I didn't have a knife so I dug into the pot with my finger and spread the jam as best I could over the crumbly cake. Then I divided it into six and shared out all the other food too. We didn't have a tablecloth for anything but the floor seemed perfectly clean.

'So come on then, let's eat!'

We sat down around the feast and felt for the food.

'Yuck, it's all sticky,' said Karen.

'I'm not hungry,' said Louise. 'This food is disgusting.'

I didn't really feel hungry either but I took a big bite of cake just to show her. It felt a bit funny at first—but after a few bites my tummy woke up.

'How weird, I'm really starving,' I said, chomping cake for all I was worth. 'I like this cake with jam. It's like real jam sponge now. I wonder if I ate it with a bit of Yorkie it would taste like chocolate sponge?' I experimented. 'It's lovely! You try, you lot. It's as good as Black Forest gateau, really.'

They all tried, even Louise, and everyone agreed it was incredible. I took a handful of Janie's salt and vinegar crisps and added them to my current mouthful.

'And now it tastes like Black Forest gateau and chips! Utterly delicious.'

Only Rosemary believed me this time.

'She'll be sick, Stella,' said Marzipan reproachfully.

'No I won't. It's lovely, delicious, just like Stella says,' Rosemary insisted, feeding the same mixture to Dora. 'Dora likes it too. Look at her gobbling it up.'

The crisps and chocolate made me desperately thirsty. Janie and Rosemary had been sipping at their lemonade all day and it had already gone flat. I tried a couple of mouthfuls but it didn't help.

'I'm just nipping along to the bathroom,' I said, getting up. 'I'm so thirsty.'

'You shouldn't drink the water out of the taps, it's bad for you,' said Marzipan.

'I like things that are bad for me,' I said. 'You are an old fusspot, Marzie-Parzie.' I bent and tickled her. 'Fuss, fuss, fuss,' I said, my fingers scrabbling.

Marzipan shrieked.

'Stop it! Stella, please stop it, I can't stand being tickled, stop it!' Marzipan giggled hysterically.

I tickled harder. Marzipan was sitting cross-legged. She suddenly toppled over right into the food, landing with her nose in the jammy cake crumbs. We all shrieked with laughter.

I could still hear them laughing when I was in the bathroom. And I could hear something else too. That wailing noise. It went on and on and it sounded so sad.

It was no use. I simply had to find out what it was.

Chapter Fourteen

I crept along the corridor, trying to kid myself I wasn't scared. I could hardly see a thing. I edged along the wall, feeling my way, and then gasped. Something soft and feathery flickered across my face. I swotted at it violently and found myself holding bits of leaves. I'd been attacked by one of Miss Hamer-Cotton's potted plants, that was all. I rather suspected I'd done it a serious damage but there wasn't time to be bothered about it now.

I could still hear the faint wailing. It lured me onwards. I longed to go back for the others but I badly wanted to show off to Karen that I'd gone by myself.

I got to the end of the corridor and turned right. The wailing was louder now, although it stopped every now and then as if it was pausing for breath. I was pretty breathless myself and I felt horribly sick. I still had the taste of Black Forest gateau and chips in my mouth and it didn't help at all.

I saw a light shining from under one of the

doors near the end. I stood still, listening, waiting for the next wail. When it came I was certain it was coming from that room. I crept nearer until I was standing right outside. I listened so hard my ears ached. There was someone murmuring inside and some little snuffly sounds. Then a wail and more murmurs. I couldn't quite make out whose voice it was. I sidled right up to the door, pressing my ear against the cold wood. I pressed too hard. The door burst open and I hurtled into the room.

There was a startled yowling and scrabbling from the bed. Orange Overall was sitting there with her hair in pink plastic curlers and her eyes all peepy with fatigue. Well, actually she was Nylon Nightie tonight, hyacinth blue, with pretty pink ribbons to match her curlers. She wasn't doing the yowling and scrabbling herself. She was holding something in her arms, wrapped in an old towel. The something was very small and soft and snuffling. It wailed pathetically, sounding panic-stricken.

'What are you playing at, you naughty girl,' Nylon Nightie hissed. 'You frightened us out of our wits.' She peeped into the towel. 'Sh, pet, calm down now. It's just a great silly girl. Nothing to be frightened of. There, just as I'd got you sorted out and sleepy. I don't know.' She patted the towel soothingly and then looked at me properly.

'Oh my goodness, whatever have you done to yourself?' She abandoned the towel and sprang out of bed. 'Where does it hurt? Have you told Miss Hamer-Cotton? We'd better call the doctor quick.'

I stared at her, baffled.

'A doctor? Why? What's the matter?' I stammered.

Nylon Nightie gestured dramatically at my front. 'Look at the blood!'

I looked. It was not a pretty sight. My nightie was streaked with scarlet. I stared at it, wondering how I could be bleeding to death without it hurting—and then I wet my finger and licked the red.

'It's strawberry jam.'

'Jam? How—?'

'What's wrapped in that towel?' I said very quickly indeed.

I darted round Nylon Nightie and got to the bed. The towel was wriggling furiously and giving intermittent wails. I found a corner and pulled. A little red furry animal was exposed, its big brown eyes glinting, black snout quivering.

'Oh how lovely,' I whispered. 'Isn't it sweet. Is it . . . is it a kitten or a puppy?'

'He's a fox cub,' said Nylon Nightie, and she sat on the bed and picked him up. He nuzzled into her nylon folds, his thick tail neatly wrapped round his tiny body. He wailed again, but Nylon Nightie stroked him and whispered to him soothingly until he was quiet.

'Where did you get him?' I said.

I decided I wanted a fox cub for a pet more than anything else in the whole world.

'I found him out near the dustbins. I think the mother fox must have led all her cubs there. We've had foxes foraging around in the bins for a while. Right little nuisances they are. Did you hear that, you cheeky little chap?' She shook her head at him fondly. 'Anyway, this little fellow got left behind. He'd cut his paw on a tin can and couldn't run properly. He was crying his eyes out and I couldn't resist him. I knew he didn't have much chance if I left him where he was. So I took him indoors and I've had him here with me now a couple of weeks or more. His paw's nearly better now so I can let him go soon—and it won't be before time. You haven't half led me a dance, haven't you, my boy?' She sighed. 'Did you hear him having a little whimper, is that why you're here?'

'I've heard him several times. I couldn't think what it could be. What's the matter with him? Is his paw hurting to make him wail like that?'

'No, I think he's fine. He just wants to be up and about. Foxes stay up all night in the wild, don't they? This little fellow just wants to play and when I put my head down on the pillow he starts making a right fuss until I give in to him.'

'I'll play with him,' I said eagerly. 'Can I stroke him?'

'Gently then. And mind his teeth. He can't half nip even at this age.'

I touched his soft fur. He quivered as I gently smoothed it. I could feel his blood beating under his skin.

'He's so beautiful,' I said. 'He doesn't mind me stroking him, does he? Imagine, I'm stroking a real live fox! Wait till I tell the others.'

'Oh no! You're not to tell anyone,' said Nylon

Nightie sharply. 'It's a secret, Stella, do you hear me? If Miss Hamer-Cotton gets to know about little Foxy here she'll go spare. You know what she's like about that silly Stinky-tinky cat of hers.'

I giggled.

'If Stinkypoo caught one whiff of this little chap he wouldn't half throw a tantrum. Miss Hamer-Cotton would get rid of Foxy before you could blink. So I've got to keep him secret until he's old enough to be set free.'

'Couldn't I even tell my best friend Marzipan?'

'No, I know what you kids are like. Your friend will tell someone else and soon the whole lot of you will know and then there'll be nudges and giggles and Foxy jokes and it'll be all round Evergreen. I've got my job to think of, haven't I?'

'I suppose so. But we wouldn't tell, honestly.'

'I know you wouldn't mean to. But I still want you to keep quiet, all right? You won't even tell your pals in your dormi?'

'All right. I promise. I won't breathe a word,' I said, sighing.

It would have been so wonderful to boast about Foxy to Karen and Louise but it couldn't be helped.

'I'll only have him a few days more anyway,' said Nylon Nightie, and she reached out and patted him regretfully.

'Can't you keep him? Make him a proper pet?'

'Oh no, that wouldn't be fair. Foxes are meant to be wild. And he's getting a right handful already. He keeps getting into scrapes.' She gave me a funny sideways look. 'I suppose I might as well tell you now. It was Foxy who chewed up your nice story book.'

'He didn't!'

'Although it was really my fault, I suppose. I shouldn't have let him out of my room. But he gets so cooped up in here all day and all night that he tears round chasing his own tail, going barmy for lack of exercise. He makes such a mess, you wouldn't believe. I thought it might calm him down a bit if I took him for a little walk. So I took him with me when I vacuumed all the dormis, using my dressing gown cord as a sort of lead. So there I was, cleaning your dormi with Foxy safely tied to the bedpost, or so I thought. But the little devil wriggles free, doesn't he, and gets his head into your chest of drawers and mistakes your book for a big bite of dinner.'

'You bad little boy,' I said, pretending to tap Foxy on the back. 'Oh well. It's all mended now, so it doesn't really matter.'

One thing mattered. I'd been so sure Karen had spoilt my book. I'd said some awful things to her. She'd cried all night—and it hadn't been her fault after all.

I felt hot and fidgety when I thought about it. I'd have to try to make it up to her somehow. But I didn't want to think about it now. I concentrated on Foxy instead.

'Do you think I could actually have him on my lap for a minute?' I asked.

'I don't see why not. Go gently though.'

I lifted him and cradled him almost like a baby. He whined and scrabbled a bit, but I held on to him and begged him to be a good boy—and he suddenly stopped trying to get away.

'He's snuggling into me, look! He likes me,' I whispered.

'Mind he doesn't pee on you. He's worse than a baby,' said Nylon Nightie, chuckling.

I remembered Dora's bed and the damp patch and knew who was the culprit!

'I wish we could keep him,' I said wistfully. 'Couldn't we make some sort of cage for him?'

'You wouldn't like to be cooped up in a cage, would you? Well, neither would he.'

'But how's he going to manage when you let him go again? Do you think he'll be able to find his mother?'

'Maybe. Yes, I expect she'll come when she hears him wailing. He's obviously been missing her a lot.'

'I miss my mum,' I said.

'Of course you do, pet,' said Nylon Nightie, and she put her arm round me. 'Still, she'll be coming to collect you soon. And you're having a good time here, aren't you?'

'Well. Sometimes,' I mumbled.

'You'd better get back to your dormi now, eh? It's ever so late. And remember, you'll keep quiet about Foxy, won't you?'

I kept my word—although it was agony. The others were all desperate to know where I'd been. Rosemary was *crying*, and Marzipan had been all set to go and tell Miss Hamer-Cotton I was missing.

'You mad twit! You couldn't tell on me, you're supposed to be my friend,' I said indignantly.

'Well, I was so worried about you. You weren't in the bathroom. We looked all over the place for you but you'd just disappeared.'

'So where did you go, Baldy? You didn't hear that wailing noise again, did you?' asked Karen.

'What wailing noise?' I said vaguely. 'No, I didn't hear any noise. I just decided to go for a little walk, so I did.'

'In the pitch dark?'

'Mmm. I dared myself.'

'You're *mad*, Baldy,' said Karen—but she sounded a little bit impressed.

Chapter Fifteen

I got another parcel from Mum and Uncle Bill the next day. They were in Italy now so they'd sent me a gilt gondola crammed with chocolate lire coins and a new T-shirt. I thought the gondola was very grand but I'd rather gone off chocolate since the midnight feast, so I wondered about offering it as a prize for my Super Star magazine quiz. I'd had a lot of entries, mostly because I'd promised a Super Star prize for the winner, and I was getting a bit bothered about what it was going to be.

I certainly didn't want to donate my new T-shirt. It was emerald green with silver stars patterned all over it. I loved the stars although I was a bit sick of Emerald green. Louise pointed out the designer label and actually seemed impressed. Karen said nothing but she looked at my T-shirt longingly.

Karen didn't have any nice T-shirts of her own. She had the giveaway Evergreen one and some old baggy things that had gone out of shape.

Some girls wouldn't bother about it but Karen cared desperately about clothes.

I still hadn't made it up to Karen for thinking that she'd ripped my book.

I thought it over. I shuffled several thoughts.

'I think I'll keep my gondola and offer my new Italian T-shirt as the Super Star prize,' I said.

'You're mad, Baldy,' said Karen. 'Giving away that fabulous T-shirt! What if someone like James wins it? He couldn't even get it over his big fat head—and anyway, it would be wasted on a boy.'

'So why don't you try and win the T-shirt for yourself?' I suggested.

'I'm not doing your daft competition,' said Karen. 'Besides, I can't, can I? The Emerald girls aren't allowed to enter because we made up some of the questions.'

'You didn't,' I said. 'You wouldn't join in. So I can't stop you entering, can I?'

So Karen bought a copy of the magazine and got busy. She handed in her competition entry the next morning. She'd made heaps of silly guesses. She didn't really do very well at all. But I was the editor and I was the one who marked all the entries.

'You'll never guess who's won,' I announced at the end of the week.

Karen put on her new emerald green starry T-shirt and stared at herself in the mirror. Her eyes were as shiny as the stars.

'Even Louise hasn't got a T-shirt as posh as this,' she said softly. 'You're mad to give it away, Baldy, but thanks all the same.'

Marzipan grinned at me.

'That was ever so good of you, Stella,' she said privately.

I got a bit unnerved. I was used to being bad, not good. And yet I seemed to have got into the habit of being good now. I didn't muck about so much in all the activities and Jimbo said I was practically black belt standard at judo now, although he might have been joking.

I'd made friends with Miss Hamer-Cotton and coloured her a big picture of Tinkypoo. She was very pleased with it and pinned it up on her wall, although she said it was a pity about the little orange smudge. It wasn't a smudge. It was a very very tiny picture of Foxy with his teeth bared ready to bite Tinkypoo in a very rude place indeed—but of course I didn't explain that.

I was even making progress in macramé. I got Jilly to show me how to make a watchchain. It just looked like a long piece of tangled string when I'd finished, but when I gave it to the Brigadier and explained what it was he seemed delighted. I

153

wondered about making a watchchain for Uncle Bill too because they were really easy to do, but I decided against the idea. I set about making myself a wig instead.

'I'm going to start a new fashion. String hair! You don't have to wash it or comb it so it's a great improvement on the real thing. And you can wear little brown paper bows for the complete parcel look,' I said, plaiting away.

The others all thought I was mad but Jilly said it was a very original idea.

But I still couldn't swim. I did try. But I knew it wasn't going to work.

'I *can't* do it, Uncle Ron. Can't we just give up?' I said, struggling, desperate to keep my head out of the water. I was still so scared of going under.

'You're *nearly* swimming. If you could just stop being so scared and start to enjoy it then you'd be swimming like a little fish,' said Uncle Ron. 'You can't expect to swim when you're all tense and terrified.'

That was daft: I was all tense and terrified because I couldn't swim. It was no use. Uncle Ron found me a cork float but it kept bobbing away with me and I couldn't bear it. He tried me doing doggypaddle instead of the breast stroke but that was even worse, because when I splashed the water went right up my nose.

'Come *on*, Stella, there's a chum,' said Uncle Ron, screwing up his face in frustration. 'I was so sure we'd have you swimming by now. Just six little strokes, eh? Then we can put you in for the Beginners race in the swimming gala.'

Janie and Bilbo and all the other beginners could do at least six strokes by now. I couldn't do one. So I was the only child at Evergreen who didn't take part in the gala.

'As if I care,' I said airily.

'You are a *baby* though, Baldy,' said Karen. 'Fancy not being able to swim when even a little kid like Bilbo can do it, easy-peasy.'

Sometimes I very much regretted letting her have that T-shirt.

The star of the swimming gala was Alan. Uncle Ron had let him go in the advanced team after the first week. He won all the races. It really annoyed Louise. It really pleased me. Uncle Ron got him to give a diving display at the end of the gala and the Brigadier presented him with a special little trophy.

The Emeralds got so many team points for swimming that we won the Evergreen trophy too.

'Although it's no thanks to you, Stella Stebbings,' said Louise, still cross because she'd only come second at swimming. 'You kept losing us all those rotten team points by messing about and being so stupid.'

'Cheek! I won some of them back. Miss Hamer-Cotton gave me two for my magazine, so there.'

'Now then, now then,' said Miss Hamer-Cotton, shaking her head at us. 'I don't want to see any cross faces today. Why don't you all hurry over to Jimbo and Jilly? They're fixing a special camp fire feast and I'm sure they could do with a bit of help cooking the sausages.'

'Ooh, yummy! I love sausages,' I said, starting to run—but the Brigadier beckoned me.

'Miss Stebbings? Might we have a little word?'

So the others all rushed off without me.

'I was disappointed not to see you in the pool with all the other children,' said the Brigadier.

'I *said* I wouldn't ever be able to swim.'

'Did you really try?'

'Yes! Really. But it's no use.'

'Uncle Ron says you *could* swim. You just worry about getting water on your face.'

'I don't like going under.'

'You won't, not if you swim. And even if you do, it's all right so long as you're in the shallow end. You can just bob up again.'

'I still know I can't swim.'

'And I know you can. Tell you what. How about giving it one more try now?'

'No thank you.'

'As a little present for me?'

'I've already given you a present.'

The Brigadier laughed and felt in his waistcoat pocket. He produced his half hunter watch on the end of my grubby macramé chain.

'And it's proving very useful, as you can see. But I'd really like you to try to swim too. Will you?'

I sighed. 'I haven't got my swimming costume.'

'It won't take you two minutes to nip back to the house to get it. And tell you what. I'll come too and I'll get mine. We'll have a little swim together, all right?'

I still wasn't keen, but I rather wanted to see what the Brigadier looked like in his swimming costume. I hoped he'd look really funny in one of those old stripy suits that come right down past the knees. But he had a pair of perfectly ordinary navy trunks and he didn't look funny in them at all, just a bit white and wrinkly.

'You promise you won't throw me in?' I said, shying away from him when he tried to take hold of my hand.

'Of course I won't. You make your own way down the steps. I'll just get in and get warm.'

He dived in. It was quite a good dive too, almost Alan standard. He swam up and down the pool in a flash.

'You can swim ever so fast even though you're old,' I said, when he came up to me at the steps.

'I'm not sure whether I should be flattered or cross,' he said, laughing. 'Well, are you getting in properly, young lady? You're shivering.'

'I know. I don't want to. I hate swimming.'

'Come on, Miss Stebbings, don't lose all your spirit,' he said encouragingly.

So I went down one step and then another and stood in the cold water and screwed up my face and slid forward and *tried* to swim. I really tried. I pushed with my arms and I kicked with my legs but the moment I started moving I panicked. I tried to put my head back so it wouldn't get wet and my feet bumped on to the ground.

'See. It's no use. And Uncle Ron's tried me with a float and tried me with doggy-paddle and tried holding me under the chin but nothing works,' I said despairingly.

'Has he tried backstroke?' said the Brigadier.

'What's that?' I said suspiciously.

So the Brigadier flipped over on to his back and showed me.

'It's fun,' he shouted. 'The water doesn't get in your face this way. You don't have to do the armstroke. You can just paddle your hands like this. You'll stay up in the water so long as you kick your legs.'

'I couldn't do that!'

'Have a go. Look, I'll hold the back of your

head. I won't let you go under, I promise. You just lie back in the water. It's like a big comfy bed, you'll see. Then just kick your feet, paddle your hands—and Bob's your uncle.'

'My uncle's Bill, not Bob,' I muttered.

'My, what a girl for a quibble. Come on then. Over on to your back. I've got you. You're perfectly safe, I promise. Come on now, Stella. Give it a try.'

So I leant back into the water. The Brigadier cupped the back of my head with his big gentle hands. I kicked up with one leg and kicked up with the other too.

'That's it. Stick the old tummy out, that'll help keep you up. Keep kicking with legs. Gently, you don't have to do the tarantella. And paddle with your hands. There. That's it! You're swimming, Stella. You're swimming!'

I was! All right, he still had hold of my head—but only just. I was very nearly swimming all by myself. It wasn't fun, it was still as scary as ever, but I was actually doing it.

We practised for ten minutes. Well, the Brigadier said it was ten minutes. It felt more like ten hours to me.

'I can smell sausages,' he said at last. 'Perhaps you'd better run along now. How about just one more go though? Without me this time?'

'No!' I said.

But I tried again. It was much worse without his hands. But at least I wasn't splashing water in my face. In fact if I stared up at the sky I couldn't see the water at all. So I kicked and I paddled and I counted. One, two, three, four, five, six. As quickly as I could. Then I put my feet down.

'I did it!' I yelled. 'I swam six strokes, didn't I? Well, sort of six.'

'Undoubtedly six,' said the Brigadier, beaming. 'Well done! You can go and eat six sausages now in celebration.'

So I wrapped myself in my towel and ran off to join the others.

'Guess what! I swam. I really swam. Ask the Brigadier if you don't believe me. I swam, Karen, so take it back about me being a baby. I swam six strokes all by myself, so there! Here, I hope you greedy lot have saved me some sausages.'

I didn't eat six. I ate *seven*. I even beat James. Evergreen really wasn't so bad after all. I could swim. I'd produced a magnificent magazine. And I was the sausage-eating star of the whole camp.

But I didn't tell Mum and Uncle Bill when they came to collect me the next day. It took me ages saying goodbye to everyone. I gave Marzipan and Rosemary and Janie a big hug and I waggled my tongue at Karen and Louise. I said goodbye to all the Emerald boys too and Alan gave me his last

week's copy of the *Beano*. I found Orange Overall and gave her a handful of my chocolate lire coins to share in secret with Foxy. I gave Uncle Ron a wave. I shook hands demurely with Miss Hamer-Cotton. I even tried to stroke Tinkypoo but he hissed and ran away. And I asked the Brigadier to bend right down and then I gave him a kiss. He went very pink and I think he was pleased.

'I hope you come back next year, Stella,' he said.

I smiled because I wanted to be polite for once.

Uncle Bill could barely conceal his triumph.

'What did I tell you?' he chortled, when we were in the car. 'I knew you'd love Summer Camp, Stella. I was right, wasn't I?'

'No. You were not right at all. You were wrong, wrong, wrong,' I insisted.

Mum leant over and gave me a hug.

'Come off it, darling. You've obviously been having the time of your life. And you've made all these new friends. Which one was Marzipan? Was she the one with the ponytail wearing the T-shirt we sent you? Did you give it to her as a goodbye present? That was nice of you.'

'That was Karen. I had to give her the T-shirt,' I muttered.

'Why? Did you do a swap with her? Oh, Stella,

I'm so glad you had a good time. I couldn't help worrying about you at first,' said Mum.

I wanted her to go on worrying about me. And I wanted Uncle Bill to stop chortling.

'I keep telling you, I didn't have a good time. It was *terrible*. I was just pretending when I said goodbye. They were all hateful to me. That girl Karen, she *made* me give her my T-shirt. And she messed up all my things. She even stole my chocolate. They were all horrid to me and they teased me about my hair.'

'I can't imagine anyone getting away with teasing you, Stella,' said Uncle Bill.

'What did they say about your hair?' said Mum. 'It looks a lot better now it's grown a bit. It's still rather spiky but it looks cute. I think it suits you.'

I was beginning to get used to it myself but I wasn't going to let them know that.

'They called me Baldy and they all laughed at me. It was awful. The whole camp was awful. And they made me go in the swimming pool, I *told* you they would. Every single day. It was a special punishment.'

'Why were you being punished?' said Mum.

'Oh they just kept picking on me,' I said quickly. 'And the food was disgusting, they half starved us.'

I decided the seven sausages for supper didn't count.

'So I take it you don't want to go back next year after all?' said Mum.

'You must be joking,' I declared. 'I only just managed to survive it this time.'

Troublesome Angels and Flying Machines
Hazel Marshall
ISBN 978-0-19-275442-4

Blanco can't believe it! Count Malefico has invited him to visit. He's finally going to fulfil his lifelong dream and build a flying machine. Maybe, if he's really lucky, the Count might even let him fly it.

Eva can't believe it either! How could her parents send her off to Spain to be married to a man old enough to be her grandfather? Anyway, why does she have to have horrid Aunt Hildegard to accompany her? After all, she's got her very own angels to keep her out of trouble...

Eva thinks Blanco's wonderful—her hero. But Blanco just thinks Eva is bonkers...

'Intelligently written and a real page-turner.'   *Birmingham Post*

'a charming and highly readable fancy'   *TES*

Pippi Longstocking
Astrid Lindgren
ISBN 978-0-19-275413-4

Pippi is nine years old. She lives alone in her own house with a horse and a monkey, and she does exactly as she pleases. She has no mother and she believes her father is the king of a cannibal island. She has never learnt to look after herself and has never been to school. Her friends Tommy and Annika are green with envy—but although they have to go to school and go to bed when they are told, they still have time to join Pippi on all her great adventures.

Clubbing Together
Helena Pielichaty
ISBN 978-0-19-275430-0

Meet the fabulous, fun, feisty girls...

Sammie – The girl who turned into a big fat liar (but whose pants *didn't* catch fire).
Brody – The model from the States (who's in a bit of a state herself).
Alex – The girl with the voice of an angel (who can be a little devil too).
Jolene – The runaway who's trying to do a good turn (just make sure she doesn't turn on you).

These are the girls from ZAPS After School Club and each has their own story to tell. They all have very different lives and all have families who can be a complete pain in the you-know-where—but through all their ups and downs they have a common bond... even when they're not the best of friends.

All the girls come back again in:

Clubbing Again
ISBN 978-0-19-276348-8

Sammie – All she wants is for her family to be together for Christmas— that's not too much to ask, is it? But when she tries to put a plan into action, everything goes pear-shaped and things end up a complete disaster. Poor Sammie—will she ever be able to get it right?
Brody – The sassy model is fed up with everyone depending on her— Brody the Reliable. And when things start falling apart and she needs a bit of support, nobody wants to know—not even her boyfriend. Well, enough's enough—from now on Brody's looking after number one.

The girls have certainly got their fair share of problems—friends, family, school—nothing ever goes smoothly. But at least they have the After School Club where they can hang out with their friends and relax... well, most of the time.

Jacqueline Wilson trained as a journalist on leaving school, but started writing freelance after having her daughter Emma. She is now one of the best-selling children's writers—over 13 million copies of her books have been sold in the UK alone. She has won the Smarties Prize, Children's Book of the Year at the British Book Awards, and the Guardian Children's Fiction Award.

Jacqueline lives in a small house in Kingston crammed with 10,000 books. Every day she swims fifty lengths before breakfast, works on her stories, telephones her daughter, writes many letters to fans, and goes to bed with a book.